Landings:
Frivolous and Serious

Joseph PJ Westlake

Copyright 2020
Joseph PJ Westlake

ISBN: 9798639938658

WARNING TO WOULD-BE READERS

This is not an infants' primer.

There are tales of both fact and fiction – some of which, taken ex-contextually, have the potential to induce, in the more sensitive reader, the condition known in Victorian Britain as 'the vapours.' (Where did I put the sal volatile?)

1. Some of the following twenty-one stories are factual, taken from the memoirs of an unusual sixty years of marriage. *
2. Others are fictional, emanating from an (some have said) over-active imagination.
3. Yet others derive from the metaphysical and esoteric.

There are those who have registered their (sadly to be regretted) inability to differentiate between 2 and 3.
You, dear Reader, I am sure, will find no such difficulty.

If these cautionary words have caused you any feelings of unease,

PUT THE DAM' BOOK BACK ON THE SHELF AND GO BACK TO SLEEP!

All financial proceeds from this publication will be allocated without deduction to African children's charities, as are the proceeds from all my literary publications.

*For the full story see *A MARRIAGE: Travel, Spiritualism and Dementia*, by Joyce Westlake and Joseph PJ Westlake.
Available from Amazon/Kindle as download or paperback.

ACKNOWLEDGEMENT

It would be most remiss of me not to acknowledge unreservedly, the invaluable collaborative support of my two 'ghosts', Sue and Steve Rollins (of this parish), (I withdraw, with not inconsiderable experiential authority on the subject, the appellation 'ghosts' to replace it, equally unreservedly (!), with 'substantive authorities on matters literary and linguistic,') across whom I had the great good fortune to chance in my eighty-eighth (or was it eighty-seventh?) year and to both of whom (also I hasten to add, indeed to you, dear Reader), since they were required to grapple with sometimes unusual and contentious religio-philosophical issues not often encountered in a simple anthology, I deign the right to some reservation of credulity in the face of the, occasionally, incredible; so that what started as a sort of valued pseudo- (at least on my part) professional partnership developed, over a few short (after eighty-nine of them, all years are short) years, into an even more valued friendship.

Thanks guys.

Joseph P J Westlake
Tywyn, Gwynedd.
January 2020

CONTENTS

THE SKIRL O' THE PIPES

I recall times when we'd park for the night by one of those magnificent seascapes or loch and mountain views for which the area is famous. The notorious Scotch mist and drizzling rain would enfold us. Then we'd sit tight, perhaps for days at a time, enjoying the kaleidoscopic changes in the scenery as the clouds swept down around us only to lift again at the whim of the fickle winds.

Sometimes during those waits for the weather to clear we might not see or hear another human for days. A few sheep bleating as they came grazing by, or a flock of hoodies cawing past on the blustering gale. A small flotilla of Eider, bobbing and cooing in the surf. At dusk, those gut-wrenching moments when the red-throated and black-throated divers renewed their inconsolably grieving conversations across the lochs and lochans, with perhaps a curlew adding its own poignant counterpoint.

Or a never-to-be-forgotten dusk when, with the light fast fading under lowering clouds, borne on the evening breeze came the indescribably haunting skirl of a lone piper. Playing, I guessed, simply for his own pleasure – or, judging by the evocative, emotional stirring of my own heart strings – perhaps trying to assuage his own inner grief over a loss – he sat on the gunwale of his rowboat, a quarter mile away across the sea-loch. The moving melody, modulated by its own echo from the towering Torridon massif looming behind us, brought us to our feet.

With tears smarting our eyes, we hugged, heart to heart.

*

EVEN IN PINK

I'm dressed in a completely inappropriate shade of pink. I don't really like the hang of my dress, either, though it does accentuate the smooth slenderness of my hips and the sleek roundness of my buttocks.

It's only a few months since I came out as transvestite. My raven black hair has grown beautifully to shoulder length. I still carry a noticeable five-o-clock shadow that necessitates twice-daily shaving as well as the judicious application of suitably subtle cosmetics; and I usually stick to more muted shades when joining the group's monthly meetings.

Business associates Sylvester/Sheila and Harvey/Hilary sponsored me but I don't really fit. I've seen the secretive glances between the others; furtive whispers, sidelong smiles tell me much more than could any words. Sometimes their muttered whisperings stay with me into the night, driving me mad. They're all about the same, I reckon. No-one's really interested in me – even in bloody pink.

Bunch of self-centred, self-opinionated, stuck-up, egotistical, narcissistic bastards. Mark/Marcia, Bob/Roberta and Mike/Michelle are the worst. They don't even try to hide their hostility. Last time they'll see me here, that's for sure.

But hang on! I'll show 'em. By the time I've finished with those three… I'll cook something up and we'll have a real party – the party to end all parties – for some. My *basso profundo* chuckle is deeply resonant in my chest. I'll cosy up to them a bit, show 'em what a good time girl I really am. All new territory for me but they pretend to think I've got what it takes. I fix a date for my birthday party – at my weekend cottage. Just Marcia, Roberta and Michelle – and me.

It's as I make my purchase from the man selling bananas at the market stall that the whiff of his B-52's T-shirt, a heady homogeny of sweat, fruit, and chicken masala, reminds me. The taste and aroma of a good, strong Indian will easily cover the undertone of pulverised laburnum seeds.

I know about these things because my dear gypsy mother taught me the secrets long known to her forbears. She used to chant verses in her unique Romani lilt to instil her traditional wisdom into my receptive young mind. It's been a while so I've lost the lingo, but it goes roughly like this.

When young, my Mum scolded, watch out what you eat!

I can't have you dropping down dead at my feet.

Some leaves you can chew and some berries are tasty.

Others are horrible, flavours most nasty.

Foxglove's digitalis can kill or can cure.

Deadly Nightshade bears berries. Fatal
for sure.

Berries that paralyse nerves in blood
vessels,

Also the   heart   and   intestinal
muscles.

There was another verse about the toxicity of laburnum which I'll not repeat for fear of incriminating myself!

But it's worked! It's bloody worked!

Mark/Marcia is the last to succumb. She lies on her back across the still-twitching bodies of her buddies. Her fluttering arms stretch out towards me, her oscillating eyeballs seek sympathy. I am implacable.

The sound of the evidence-disposing dishwasher muttering away quietly in the kitchen provides a delicate counterpoint to the magnificent guitar and percussion work of the Dire Straits track on the hi-fi and the diminishing drumming of Marcia's heels on the light oak parquet of the lounge floor as she writhes in her death throes. The rattle of her final convulsion coincides impeccably with the concluding, crashing, Chad   Cromwell   cymbals   and Mark Knopfler guitar chords from the CD … and the dishwasher's fading, ululating murmur.

The silence is – silent. No more whirring, whining, white noise in my head. No more silky sibilants from voices whose tantalising whispers I could never quite catch. I'm free.

The day Sylvester/Sheila brought Harvey/Hilary into my office went down earlier in my mind as the most disastrous of my short-lived incursion into the female psyche. But now it's all over. Or it will be when I've eliminated them, too.

I'm back to my life as a heavily bearded (I think I'll keep my hair long) cynical, egotistical gentleman viticulturist from a minority group. Which is all I've always, really, ever wanted to be.

Jekyll? Hyde? Man, they've got nothing on me.

The grapes, I must say, are looking especially good this year.

Here, try a couple. Jack – sorry Jackie.

What do you think?

Should be a good vintage, I reckon.

Yeah. Kushti bok, Gorja.

Good luck to you too, pal.

*

ALL LIFE'S A GAMBLE

I had an acquaintance, let's call him Mr G, living in Wimbledon, who'd made lots of money as a professional gambler in both racing and backgammon. So successful had he been that all the regular bookmakers had blacklisted him – they wouldn't accept his horseracing bets. It was Spring of 1990. At the time I was, comparatively though not voluntarily, a gentleman of leisure and had accrued some savings. Although I'd started going to the races with my father around the age of seven, I'd followed Dad's lessons all my life, for he was a good man and didn't gamble. But – why not have a go now? Together, Mr G and I figured a way; not so much a system as a method. Not so much a pleasure as a discipline.

We would bet on nearly every race at all the day's meetings. I installed a second telephone and opened accounts with the ten leading bookmakers of the day – all the ones who had banned Mr G. For up to four hours each day, sometimes six days a week, I would keep the phone lines open, a telephone at each ear, one for Mr G and the other for ringing the bookies. Mr G had subscribed to a closed-circuit TV system displaying up-to-the minute odds at each day's meetings, and we calculated our bets from that data. This was, at that time, what some bookmakers did, combining this data with personal knowledge and help from 'insiders'. I placed multiple bets across bookmakers selected for each race. This went on for nine months, during which time I placed bets to the total value of £90,000, an average of £10,000 each month. Won some, lost some.

Then, out of the blue, one of the leading individual bookies, a name still on the TV racing programmes decades later, phoned me personally and said he would no longer accept my bets. I prevaricated momentarily before asking him why, as we'd always settled our monthly account promptly, according to which of us owed the other.

"Yes, he said, "no problem there, but you always seem to be on all the hot horses, and every day at that."

"Well, yes," I agreed, "my old granny from Lambourn left me a special hatpin for picking winners."

He laughed long and loud. "I've already connected your name with Lambourn so I've a good idea who you are. It's been nice knowing you," he said, "but sorry, no more bets. I'll settle your account at the end of the month and then it's closed."

I told Mr G who sighed and said, "Well it was bound to happen. He'll talk to the others and they'll all close us down. Best balance things between us and be happy to have had some fun with them."

I'd agreed with Joyce on a fixed limit of £4,000 which I'd commit to this gambling spree. If I lost that, I'd close it down. Maximum winnings on any one day had hit £11,000, and there were times I was over £20,000 ahead, but even that thrill didn't last. At the end, I was nearly £3,000 pounds down, though only as much as that because one of the smaller bookies refused to pay me the £1,100 he owed me. Under English law, gambling debts are not recoverable, and I didn't much care for the idea of pistols at dawn which, anyway, was no longer a fashionable option. It'd been an interesting and fun year and we'd lost less than the cost of a holiday.

Together Joyce and I had watched a lot of racing on television and had even gone together to a few local meetings. Back then we still knew who many of the trainers and jockeys were and we followed the fortunes of our favourites. Among them were Pat and Paul Eddery, Steve Donohue, the American Steve Cauthen, Frankie Dettori, who later famously rode all seven winners at an Ascot meeting. There was one I'd briefly sat next to in school. The school was run by my Dad's sister, Amy, in Grandad's house in Upper Lambourn, where he owned and trained a few steeplechasers. The jockey in question mentions this in his autobiography. His name – Lester Piggott.

Oh, happy days.

*

HAMISH'S HEBRIDEAN HIDEAWAY

Twenty years ago, as he'd gunned the motor of his small launch, he'd looked back at the two figures waving in the sunlight from the top of the curving flight of stone steps leading down to boathouse and jetty.

"Come back to us soon, lad," his grandfather had said, gruffly.

"Aye, soon, boy," his grandmother had whispered through her tears.

With heavy heart, he'd left them. After obtaining his Mining Engineering degree in Edinburgh he'd left the island of his birth to take up a post in the diamond-rich region of Griqualand West, an area which included some of the Cape's richest diamond fields.

Today, approaching the tiny Hebridean island from the south, the tall, bearded, broad-shouldered man at the wheel of the launch surveyed his home. He saw again why his grandfather had built the house in the lee of the massive old gnarled and wind-twisted trees that for decades had struggled to cover the promontory.

Hamish lifted his gaze. As he did so, two figures stepped out of the house and walked to the top of the steps, waving their greeting.

Until Jocelyn, they'd been the only family he'd ever known.

His mother, struggling with a complicated confinement, had desperately needed medical assistance. Challenging the savagery of a fierce Atlantic storm in their small motor launch, his distraught father had risked his own life in his disastrous effort to bring help from the mainland. Tumultuous breakers had lifted the frail craft, smashing it again and again, and with it his father, to crashing destruction against the rock-strewn beach. The dereliction of the boathouse reminded him again of the potential power of the sea and the night he'd been orphaned at birth.

With gasping breaths his mother had barely brought him alive and kicking into the world. Next day, the wreckage of the smashed craft appeared on the mainland beach. Willing hands scrambled a rescue boat. Alas, too late to save his mother.

Though he'd no memory of that time, Hamish had grown up aware of the insubstantial resonance of tragedy that had always permeated the island atmosphere. It had always been there, in the inescapable sadness in his grandmother's eyes, in her bearing. Was it a mistake? Bringing his new bride back here?

On today's easy swell, the sunshine sparkled and danced to the music of the rippling wavelets. Hamish killed the motor and allowed the mild, south-westerly breeze to drift his small craft closer to the tumbled rocks at the base of the eighty-foot cliff. No trouble landing today.

The brightness of the day sharpened the lines of the mountain backdrop, lifting his spirits to new heights. Beside him, the girl he'd married only two months before in Johannesburg smiled up at him, slipping her arm around his shoulders in a brief hug. He knew, without any words, that Jocelyn was sharing the thrill of his homecoming.

As their shoulders nudged with the gentle motion of the swell, he knew for sure it was no mistake. The look in her smiling eyes told him Jocelyn understood and shared his joy.

Tying his launch against the tumbledown remnants of the jetty, Hamish took Jocelyn's hand and together they climbed the steps. He turned to survey the smiling seascape, the scenic beauty of this, the island of his birth. Home, with all its memories; all its ghosts.

How differently the intervening years had treated his grandparents. Tall as Hamish was, his grandfather, now grey of brow and beard, still towered over him as they hugged in tearful embrace.

"I always knew you'd come back, lad," was all he said.

Grandmother turned from her new granddaughter and came quickly into his arms, burying her head against the rough tweed of his jacket.

"I always knew you'd come back, boy," was all she whispered through her joyous tears.

The years had been less kindly to her. Now frail and stooping, she clasped his shoulders with arthritis-twisted hands and strained to reach his cheek, to kiss it as she had so many times before. Before he left them – alone on their island.

His mind again in turmoil, he walked to the edge of the cliff and stared, unseeing, at the gentle surf lapping the rocks, eighty feet below. Painfully, his mind filled again with thoughts of his parents; how both had died tragically on the night of the terrible storm; the night of his arrival. Was it a mistake? Bringing his new bride back to this remote place? He knew well enough their lives here would be in stark contrast to the ambience of affluence and prosperity they'd left behind.

Over his shoulder, Jocelyn's sweet voice told him she was happily getting acquainted with her new family; his only family. The loving grandparents who'd devoted their lives to his upbringing, his education and seeing him started on his career. A hugely successful career that had taken him to the other side of the world; to the famous diamond mines of South Africa.

Leaving, back then, hadn't been easy. He knew the void he'd left in their declining years. At least he and Jocelyn could ensure their care and comfort now he was home.

As Jocelyn turned to him, their eyes locked. He saw again the look he'd seen as they'd exchanged their marriage vows, half the world away.

The look that already could haunt his dreams.

*

DID YOU SAY DELHI BELLY?

Delhi: last night of the tour.

The most expensive of several restaurants in a smart five-star hotel.

Betty, trip organiser, had taken it upon herself to pre-order dinner. For everyone. We'd been travelling through a Pacific Rim gourmet's paradise of splendid cuisine for six weeks. Hong Kong: savoury noodles; a vast array of colourful oriental vegetable dishes; delicious Dim Sums in profusion. Bangkok: exquisite, delicate Phad Thais; the most wonderful seafood we'd ever come across, surpassing even the sumptuous freshly caught seafood barbecues of Australia; brilliant salads of exotic fruits and vegetables we'd never even heard of. Japanese teppan-yaki cuisine: tempura; teriyaki; sushi. Now, we'd anticipated all the delights of Indian cooking: kormas; biryanis; tikka masala; all manner of curries.

All twenty of us took our places round the celebratory table, chairs pushed in by a phalanx of attentive waiters who napkinned us with a flourish and presented the menu for tonight, carefully typed out according to Betty's orders. All were identical.

Her choice for our final banquet: STEAK DINNER FOR EVERYONE!

My wife Joyce prefers to forget her reaction, but I think it showed her in one of her finest moments. In spite of the consequences.

"Betty," she stormed, the West Riding coming through in her lowered voice, "Betty, I did not pay all this money (a Yorkshire lass, remember) to travel God knows how many miles all the way to India for you to order me a beefsteak! Isn't India the country where the term 'holy cow' originated? Or is it 'sacred cow?'"

By now she was on her feet, leaning across the table as she overrode Betty's attempted interruptions. It was not the first confrontation between the two of them on this trip, but it was definitely the most public. Her voice was rising, her expression darkening with anger. Our party displayed a rich mixture of reactions, the waiters were alarmed, and other diners were beginning to notice that there was Trouble in Paradise.

"They're not supposed to even touch the ruddy animals, let alone kill 'em and cook 'em. I came to India expecting to eat indigenous food cooked by indigenous people. Not some American rubbish! I want to eat INDIAN! If we can't get it here then Joseph and I will go somewhere else and find our own dinner!"

After six weeks in the tropics we were all well-tanned so I was unable to detect any change in Betty's complexion but her body language was interesting. Twice she began rising to her feet only to subside under Joyce's sustained onslaught. Her eyes swivelled frantically in the direction of the anxious maître d'hôtel.

"Come on, Joseph. Talk about organising a pee-up in a brewery!" Joyce salvaged her handbag and her husband, turned from the table. By this time there'd been several muttered 'hear, hears' around the group.

"Joyce, wait, wait," called Betty. To give her her due, she gallantly retrieved the situation.

"It seems you're not alone in this. Come on, sit down. We can sort this out."

And she did. She beckoned the bobbing maître d' and explained that there had been a 'communication breakdown somewhere'. National pride overcame economic considerations: no doubt the steaks were frozen till the arrival of another, more gullible group. Some people, after all, will swallow *anything*. Menus of delicious-looking local cuisine (explanatory photos included) were distributed. The relieved waiters were helpfully explaining and describing, miming appreciative eating. Soon most were discussing, selecting and ordering in true festive spirit. A few, Betty and entourage included, stuck to steak.

And so it might all have ended in peace.

But for the consequences . . .

The bus to the airport contained more than a few travellers with expressions best described as 'thoughtful'. Oddly, they were those of us who had eaten Indian. The minute the 'seatbelts' sign was switched off there was a race for the toilets. It was a jumbo jet, there were quite a few, and they served their purpose admirably. All the way home to Heathrow Airport – a long trip that seemed much, much longer. It was, to use Naval parlance, a job for Turret A and Turret X.

I felt a measure of pity for the unfortunate ground staff whose job it was to clean up, and wished I could tip them.

There was a certain politely restrained smugness among the steak-eaters.

And Betty's expression said it all.

Joyce's had been a Pyrrhic victory . . .

*

DIAMONDS ARE FOREVER – PERHAPS

Promptly at nine, one Monday morning in 1958, I arrived at the Bradford office where I was Company Secretary, and was immediately called into the boss's office. He was sitting in his usual chair behind his vast, leather-topped partners' desk. Unexpectedly, the desk had been cleared of its usual litter of paperwork and telephones. Today, it was covered with some twenty-five or more squares of tissue paper, some opened out, a few still screwed up. On, or in, each piece of tissue lay a sparkling jewel.

"Good grief, are those diamonds?"

"Come in, Joseph, come in." said Mr E. "Close the door. I need some advice."

"Pardon? What do you mean?"

JJ, the boss's Belgian son-in-law, grinning like the proverbial Cheshire cat, took over, in his precisely enunciated English.

"Joseph, for reasons I will explain later, Mr E wishes to buy a diamond. As you know, before I joined Mr E's business, I was a diamond merchant in Hatton Garden where my family are still in the business. So, over the weekend I popped down to London to collect a few samples and today, for a change, we are going to buy a diamond."

"But I know nothing about angora rabbit hair or Moroccan camel hair or Merino wool or nylon filament, although we trade daily in these commodities. My job's just to keep track of them around the world. As for diamonds, well … I know even less …"

I was at a loss for further words as my gaze flitted from one glittering rock to the next. The few diamonds I'd seen in friends' engagement rings were minute compared with these … these …

"Nor does my father-in-law, so I am going to educate you both. Bring another chair and we will begin.

"Now, Mr E wants to spend no more than £12,000 (in 1958 you could buy a handful of smart semis in suburban Bradford for that amount) so I have brought a selection roughly in that bracket. Before we start looking at individual stones ..."

I was, in those days, passably good at mental arithmetic. There were over half a million pounds worth of diamonds casually (or so it seemed to me) strewn across my boss's desk.

Carats, colours, costs, faults. I confess that's all I remember.

Later, we went out for lunch.

After lunch the lesson continued but now we were using one of those funny little eyeglass things, a jeweller's loupe, to examine each stone and discuss the merits and prices of the four or five stones still under consideration. JJ was in his element and grew quite excited over some of them. Finally, a choice was made.

Ultimately, my only real contribution to the day's work was to write a cheque, on the business account, for £10,000. The boss signed it and we locked up and adjourned to the nearby Midland Hotel. The diamonds were safe in the office safe (oh dear, a tautology).

Over our G and Ts, Mr E and JJ explained.

Mr E, Turkish by birth, after giving his Greek fiancée an expensive diamond engagement ring, had married her and gone to live in Greece where he and various Greco-Turkish cousins conducted a profitable import/export business. When German troops invaded Greece during the Second World War, the E's Jewish race rendered it imperative they leave that country. (Many years later, I visited Greece and learned about some of the atrocities that occurred.) The aforementioned diamond engagement ring paid for their freedom and their escape to Britain where they arrived almost penniless. Mr E had made his wife an irrevocable promise. He would, one day, replace the ring. And he did, though I never saw the completed ring.

There was, alas, a very sad ending to this quite beautiful, romantic tale.

I am sorry to say that this devoted couple, already in their sixties, did not live happily ever after. Some years after I had left Mr E's business, I ran into JJ and his downcast wife. Tearfully, she told me that one night, after they had gone to bed, thieves had broken into the house – the bedroom – of Mr and Mrs E, bound and gagged them and, at knife-point, forced them to reveal the combination of the safe in which……

Severely shocked and heartbroken, both died soon afterwards.

*

A FRIENDLY PHONE CALL

Hello? This is John. Oh, hello Jean. Sorry I was in the shower when you called. Of course it was locked, what with all this social virusing stuff. Shame because there's something I want to share with you – and only you, because we've known each other quite a few years now. Over forty, I think, and I know I can rely on your discretion – it's a long time to keep a secret isn't it, and they say you can't trust the phones these days. Big Brother and all that. And I only called in for some bits of glass for the house. 1980 wasn't it? Yes, that long. Eh? Ninety next July and the kids were going to get me a ride on the footplate again, like they did for my seventieth. But now, with Convict 99 and the lockdown, that's all gone up in smoke, you might say. Get it? Smoke? Steam train? Footplate? Oh, never mind.

I need to pee but there's something I just have to share and so many people are such gossips and, in this case, discretion is of the essence – if she ever gets to know I've told you, she'll never speak to me again. Yes Matilda, of course; and you know how awkward that would be, thrown together as we are in the restrictive confines of a nursing home. Not allowed to leave our rooms and visit or anything. But she and I are the only ones here who, you know, actually still retain our communication skills. Well, I mean, can actually talk to each other. I'm pretty sure she said "engaging in social intercourse" but, you know, my hearing and that. Retired professional lady, she is. I think you know her. Yes well, Sister allows us to sit together in the foyer, two metres apart you know. I've heard of fleas that could jump six feet but that was before we went metric so I don't know about viruses… We have to shout a bit but we manage. Watch the world go by – but of course, it isn't. Going by, I mean. Yes, very sad, but what can you do?

Which is a problem because the man in the next room, poor old chap – dementia you know, eighty something. Keeps asking me if I've seen the Regimental Sergeant Major. Should have been here this morning but hasn't shown. It's his son actually, so I said if I see the RSM I'll put him in the guardhouse for AWOL. He smiled and said, Yes, sir, that would be best. Shuffles about the place with one of those fancy walker frames. Posh one with brakes and a seat and whatever. Jolly awkward if I'm trying to get some exercise on my Zimmer and we meet in the corridor. Someone has to back up and you're not supposed to go backwards because you could easily get your legs tangled. Think of the staff, running around like scalded lop cats, and two mechanical devices locked in mortal combat and me and Reuben writhing and moaning and cursing each other – no, I didn't renew mine after about eighty-seven, what with the dementia and the stress. What? No, not me. Dear Joan, bless her. No, I've still got my marbles. Anyway, you don't need a licence for a bloody Zimmer frame, you daft ….

I can't stop 'cos I'm cross-legged already. What I've been dying to tell you, 'cos, you know, we go back a'ways, don't we? Do you remember that first time, in your crappy old office? With its broken window? And you Double Glazing fitters. Yes, I still laugh about it. What? No, the broken glass, not us. No, I'd never laugh about us. Well, we've had many a … Pardon? I'd only come in for a few bits of glass and there you were. Full war paint, power dressed and all that, bashing away at your keyboard with bits chipped off your nail varnish and a stray strand of that beautiful hairdo trying to grow round the side frame of your specs like a twisting, twining tendril of old man's beard and I couldn't quite see down between… Eh? No. I most certainly was not. Tilly May was lying between the filing cabinet and the desk and she was thumping with her tail … at first, I thought it was my heart ha ha ha. Anyway, we did the business together, and well, there wasn't really any other reason to go on seeing each other when the house was finished and then Joan and I went off on our travels. Anyway, I didn't call to talk about us.

God, I'm bursting. No, you see, I suppose I could have unlocked the door this morning only, oh, yes, I was in the shower. Well, of course by myself, that was a naughty, suggestive remark, so there was nobody to unlock … Was Chris with you? And Tilly May? Does she still bark at the postman? Well, no, that would be too much. No, Sister has already threatened to smack my bottom if I don't behave and play by the rules. Oh, she is a one is Sister Kathrin. Listen, no, you mustn't tell Lisa, she'd begin to think you might be right about her father when you call me an old reprobate, which she knows I'm not, and so do you. It's just your little jokey way and I love you for it and I know you don't mean anything – well – you know. Because I've never been like that, as you well know. Good job I don't easily take offence or our friendship would have ended long ago. Of course, it could only be friendship, I realised that. After all, you were already spoken for, as they say, and I had Joan and three kids and we both had businesses to run and anyway forty years is too big a gap, so there. Yes, why I rang –

God, I must go for a leak. There's this chap, Martin. No, no, not the butcher. What? No, I was just crossing my legs 'cos, you know ... Do you still get your link of sausages from him? No, one of the Carers, helps me with showering and dressing and stuff. Keen motor cyclist he is – got four bikes. He said this morning, that what with her broken jaw and legs and impacted vertebrae and things, his partner – what? No, of course he didn't do it. She fell off when they were ... What? I don't think she'd stay with him if... Why do people have partners nowadays instead of husbands and wives? It used to be 'cause you could fiddle the tax. No, she's not. How could she do her job as a nurse with all that lot? So they've only got his income and that's minimum for four twelves a week, so he's had to sell one of his bikes. Three and a half grand he got. She's a biker too. Was. Used to go continental touring. Yes, she should get the insurance but that can take for ever... What, no, what I wanted to say, it's not about me at all, really. You know Matilda that I sit with in the front porch, don't you. Yes, her late husband had something similar –Well no it wasn't actually facial – no, facial, not fatal, what? Yes of course it was fatal, eventually, because it was his liver as well, poor chap. But not facial; it was behind his ear. Yes, ear. Huge, enormous sub-cutaneous cyst. Well that's what they thought. Post-operative skin graft. Pulled it round from his face. She had to tell them in the Care Home to make sure they shaved behind his ear otherwise his beard grew in a tuft behind as well as in front. Anyway, I can't stop here gossiping.

I need to pee. You know I mentioned Martin, the one who – yes, well he helps Matilda take a bath and, well, you see, when he dries my feet, I don't react, but Matilda squeals and giggles and wriggles – when he's drying *her* toes, not mine, you fool. No, of course I'm not there but there has to be one of the girls – no vulgarity, if you please. Well, I just thought you'd like to know because I think it's hilarious but don't you dare tell anyone. If it ever got back to Matilda she'd – well, I don't know. She can't get out of her chair, bless her, so I feel safe enough. Ha ha. But we chat all day and sneak a glass of sherry after supper most nights ... well, it was ten-year-old port but, as every hardened old toper like you and me knows – there's only so many glasses to a bottle. She'd never speak to me again if...

What? Oh to be back in Dublin with the boys, sat by the Liffey with a glass of the black stuff, enjoying a good crack with the lads. Jean! Jean! No, I said crack. Oh, no. C-r-a-c-k. It means … Jean … It … Silly woman, she's rung off. Oh well … She should get it. She knows I'm Irish.

Damn! I've wet myself.

*

DEATH BY TRYPANOSOMIASIS

I'm powerless, either to close my eyes or to avert them, as a fractional indentation appears in the skin of my left forearm. The compulsion to watch the irrevocable action that can end my life in inescapable agony is irresistible, not to mention unavoidable. The anaesthetic sedative in my system has induced paralysis of my limbs and a sensation of drowsiness, of exaggerated slow-motion. The minute tube has passed through the sparse downiness onto the warmly tanned surface. The pressure increases; the tiny depression suddenly pops up level again. I don't feel a thing.

The proboscis of a tsetse fly is disproportionately long in relation to its body; that of the riverine strain is of the order of five to seven microns shorter than that of the forest strain while that of the savannah strain is longer by a similar measure; nevertheless, all three are, indisputably, equally adequate for purpose.

In order to access its feast from my blood, this particular Congo riverine tsetse's proboscis has penetrated the epidermal layer. An injection achieving inoculation of its protozoa into the subcutaneous tissue – instant access to the capillaries carrying my lifeblood. The infection will quickly move into my lymphatic system, later into my blood stream, subsequently crossing into my central nervous system and invading my brain, leading inevitably, over a period of months, to my death. Unquestionably and irrevocably, I am doomed to a seriously disagreeable future.

After several seconds the tsetse's tiny tube withdraws. The murderous act is complete. Entomologically evolutionary processes now decree curtailment of my already relatively short lifespan. It could be a few weeks before the first symptoms will manifest; extreme lethargy, headaches, itchiness, fevers, joint pains. My half-brother, Eustace, will easily ensure no medical assistance reaches me. Helplessly under his control I will, within a few months – weeks perhaps – be dead. And no one will ever know how, or at whose hand, if indeed at anyone's hand, I contracted the infection. Yet another of his devious schemes.

As I abruptly switch my fascinated gaze, I notice that my aspiring, and, judging by the dew on his brow, actually perspiring, assassin (is the stress of his felonious ministrations affecting him to such degree?) has been watching as intently as have I, but for a markedly different reason. Unless I can access appropriate medical treatment, ideally in the next few hours, I will enter a protracted period of wastage of body and brain before dying a very unpleasant death. Eustace, bastard-with-murderous-intent that he is, will inherit the thirty-seven million pounds and the covetable Gloucestershire acreage bequeathed to me by our mutual progenitor in a highly complex testamentary jest.

A testamentary technicality cottoned onto by the misanthropic, murderous misogynist now standing over me as, with rubber-gloved hands, he meticulously, if somewhat nervously, removes the innocent instrument of his lethal intent and returns it to the security of my lab in the next room.

It isn't really about the money; I feel an inward smile begin as the cliché crosses my mind. Of course, it is. It all arises from the unfortunate quirk of character that for some twenty years has motivated one potential premeditated murder after another – all so cleverly conceived, concealed and planned that, up to now, although I've frustrated his many moves, the bastard (yes, the epithet is genetically applicable) has, due to the remote isolation of my medical practice, defied legal detection of his multiple homicidal schemes.

This time, as in times past, Eustace has erred in one, perhaps slightly obscure, detail. Slightly obscure maybe; but it should not have escaped him. Once again, I will thwart my brother's plan and continue to head the line of familial succession.

It is, our paternal grandfather claims, a long and honourable line, dating back to Henry, a fifteenth century yeoman freeholder. Our ancestor found favour with the local aristocracy and minor royalty when he provided shelter and soldiery during Owain Glyndŵr's Rebellion, as it fluctuated across the length and breadth of Wales, just over the nearby border, against the dominant and domineering English military and the Celtic collaborators and turncoats. Over the more recent century, our forebears have favoured the medical profession while preserving and enhancing the fabled family fortunes.

My inheriting of that £37,000,000, along with the title to a substantial Gloucestershire acreage, (in fee simple absolute in possession along with all buildings [actually a small village] forestry appurtenances and livestock domestic and indigenous thereon and therein at the relevant date extant [to paraphrase while preserving the legal profession's obsessive abhorrence of punctuation]) is dependent on one particular conditional clause in our eccentric grandfather's Will.

The Will, Gramps told us, by-passes our father who, in any case a couple of decades ago, disappeared somewhere in the Congo basin with his beautiful blonde partner-in-adultery, mother to my half-brother of murderous intent. Instead it leaves me the whole shebang, provided that, at the time of his death (grandfather's that is) I am a registered voter on the relevant electors' register of our home parish, and also physically present, at least at the estate if not actually in his presence, at the moment of his passing. Oh, and the estate must be my registered home address.

So perhaps that inward smile, as I come around from the mild sedative my brother slipped into my dinner wine to keep me passive during his homicidal ministrations, is not quite as rueful as it might be. Contrary to his optimistic belief that I am irrevocably separated from the nearest source of medical assistance and supplies by some thousand miles of Africa's second longest (but deepest) river, I already have the solution tucked away in the loft space above my rooms in the house (and clinic) we both occupy close to the never-ending flow of the Lualaba into the main Congo river.

It's a small glass bottle containing pentamidine 300mg solution. Not much but, with my additional two years training in, and several years practical experience of, tropical medicine, I am adequately equipped to deal with my present, potentially painful predicament. Something Eustace had no way of knowing when laying his plans. Of course, like everyone else for a thousand miles around, he's aware of the tsetse fly's predisposition to the innocent transmission of Trypanosomiasis; though he, like the majority of the sparse native populace, knows it only as African Sleeping Sickness. But he didn't follow me into med school so he's unaware of the appropriate antidotally-applicable treatment. He's also unaware that the monthly supply boat brings me a new stock of the short-shelf-lifed lifesaver. My insurance policy.

Because I witnessed, albeit unwillingly, the altogether natural behaviour of that tiny tsetse as it introduced its deadly dose to my subcutaneous tissue, I know I must inject the pentamidine before the dreaded protozoa has time to reach my central nervous system. I'm a jump ahead of the game.

For game it is. We both know – and each knows the other knows he knows – it's been going on for years. Move and counter-move in what, until now I've enjoyed, aberrantly I suppose, as a pleasurable gamble. To Eustace it's an altogether more desperate fixation: the stakes – the estate plus capital (aggregate a mere fifty or so million sterling) against my life.

A life in which my greatest highs have come, and continue to come, when I thwart yet another of my brother's murderous moves. It was a few years after our grandfather's disclosure of the contents of his Will, and the realisation of Eustace's obsession, that the cynical nature of Gramps' testamentary terminology struck me as an expression of his wayward perversity, his distorted sense of humour.

*

An hour or so later the sedative has worn off. Eustace has gone to his room, I retrieve the pentamidine from the loft. I'll do it now. I know I'll have to deal with the extensive side effects of the drug, but that's not a major problem. I realise how tired I am of our deadly duel of wits. I make up my mind how, when and where I'll terminate the tragi-comedy in which I've been a leading player through all these pathetic years.

He'll have to go …

It shouldn't be difficult. Where I practise my profession, just downstream from the confluence where the Lualaba, one of its many tributaries, feeds into the Congo River, the turbulent white water often conceals the high density of crocodiles and hippos.

Then, mercenary medic that I am, I'll return to living in the Gloucestershire countryside, home of my childhood, watching and waiting as Gramps quietly lives out his final years … or months … or … Well, I suppose that decision is within my purview, too. Hmmm. Perhaps too obvious. I can wait, just a little longer.

Now, where did I put that pentamidine phial? Swab? Syringe?

Damn, I've dropped it.

MY GOD, IT'S SMASHED!

I'm powerless, either to close my eyes or to avert them, as those few ccs of liquid lifesaver spread slowly at my feet ……

Damn you, Eustace, you murdering bastard. You needn't have done this. I always intended you to have a cut. You've finally won. You'll get the lot. The bloody jackpot. May you rot in Hell. What's that? … I rush to the window … our river launch is already pulling away from the jetty … out into the powerful Congo current … Damn him, he's had this planned all along and I've missed it. By the time Eustace reaches Gloucestershire, that tsetse's protozoa will have done their job.

I walk up the riverside track to where the waters tumultuously merge – a scene of violence and thundering noise that has mesmerisingly enthralled me for over two decades. There's a substantial sandbank sheltering a stretch of calmer water; several crocs snoozing on the sand as well as half a dozen ostensibly lounging lazily on the bank ahead of me. They're big brutes; some of them'll be hungry, I expect.

I approach noisily. One by one they slip away into the water. From the very edge I watch them as they haul out onto the sandbank and turn – watching me. Their eyes are quite large, you know. They don't blink like we do. I suddenly feel stupid as I kick off my boots. There's a big one still in the water, sinking lower, holding against the sheltered backwater current with a few swings of his massive tail. Suddenly his whole body explodes into a powering, thrusting drive, up towards me. I dive straight at him. … he'll get my head first …

*

AT HER MAJESTY'S PLEASURE

Like most coffee bars on Britain's High Streets in the mid-60s, mine catered to a young clientele. It housed a jukebox, two fruit machines, and several pintables, all using real coins. The machines were on a rental system. I got half the proceeds and the rental company took the other half. The machines got clients into my place. My coffee was good and I worked hard to create a relaxed ambience, 60s style. It was a friendly place.

The daily pattern of trade allowed me and occasional staff to enjoy a quiet start to each day. A scattering of regulars around mid-morning would enjoy pastries, buns, cupcakes, doughnuts, with a lull until a mild surge at lunchtime. All food served was bought in. Sausage Rolls. Pork Pies. Some prepacked sandwiches. Throughout the day customers grazed on various chocolate and candy bars. Espresso coffee, tea bags. I knew nothing about catering in those days – didn't need to. I can't even mention 'learning curve'.

Some shoppers might come in to rest their feet before catching their bus home. This kept the afternoons ticking over, but the bulk of the take would come from about seven pm as groups of teenagers came in for their daily fix – of pop music, one-armed bandits, cigarettes and coffee. 'Meals' were typical of the era: a patented range of dried foods. They came in freeze dried single portion packs, reconstituted by steam injector – beef & rice, chilli con carne & rice and a couple more. Hair was getting longer, skirts shorter, clothes more colourful, purple and yellow being favourites. Whether or not the cigarettes sometimes contained marijuana or other additives, I never knew and made no effort to find out.

The premises were set in unique, barrel-vaulted York sandstone cellars that reputedly had been part of the town's former gaol. It was sometimes described as reminiscent of Liverpool's Cavern, though it was much smaller. I made no effort to change the furniture as it was clear the customers had no expectations in that direction.

The lighting was in subdued colours but without any psychedelic gadgetry; the pop music was of the 60s era and suitably loud. Records on the jukebox were renewed on a monthly rotation and included The Beatles, The Who, The Rolling Stones, The Yardbirds, Manfred Mann, The Kinks, Herman's Hermits, Dusty Springfield, The Animals, The Beach Boys, Roy Orbison, Procol Harum, Bob Dylan, Simon & Garfunkel, The Mamas & the Papas and many more which will induce nostalgia in the post war generation.

The draw was the aroma from my genuine Italian espresso steam injector coffee machine, as it wafted gently up the steps to tickle the fancy of the passing pedestrians. I'm ninety next birthday, living in a nursing home, and I still access stuff from that era when I switch on my laptop, whilst awaiting my first coffee brewing in the cafetiere. Sometimes, the aroma can transport me back to that cellar.

Unfortunately, this relaxed, noisy atmosphere attracted a less reputable type of customer, mostly rowdy teenagers, which tended to discourage family trade. Occasionally, when cleaning up late into the evening or early morning, we would find the odd small pill in varying colours among the evening's debris, but I suspected this was the kids' idea of a joke. I hoped so. Looking back over the intervening half century I wonder how I could have been so naïve.

Came the day when one of my regular customers didn't come in for his mid-morning coffee. Later in the day, the buzz among the kids revealed the story. Although it was nearly sixty years ago, the names are changed.

Charlie, a tall lad in his late teens, would accompany his older friend, Harry, a scrap metal dealer, on their forays into remote areas of the local Dales. There they would identify a suitably located pylon carrying high-tension electricity cables. Climbing the pylon, they would then remove substantial lengths of the copper cable and carry it away in the back of their specially converted high speed pickup truck to destinations unnamed. Much to the annoyance of the utility company and the local constabulary.

On this day in late November there was a heavy wet mist engulfing most of Yorkshire and beyond. The sort of wet mist that condenses into droplets on exposed metals, such as copper and steel. Harry, clearly not the sharpest tool in the box, having selected a pylon, climbed up into the fog and applied his cutting tool to the coveted cable.

Later Charlie, straight-faced, described his surprise to me:

"There were this bloody great spark an' a bang an' 'Arry come down faster 'n I ever seen 'im."

Harry's descent was in fact a fall, and he lay ominously unmoving at the foot of the pylon. I nodded grimly at Charlie, agreeing it probably rated as the fastest ever descent from the top of a Yorkshire Electricity Board pylon.

Naturally enough, Charlie hoisted his friend into the back of the pickup:

"Well, I couldn't just bloody leave 'im there, could I? I were in big enough bloody trouble a'ready an' anyway, 'e mighta still been alive."

Making best use of the truck's upgraded performance, Charlie transported Harry swiftly to Skipton Hospital.

Consternation when Harry was declared D.O.A. – dead on arrival.

The subsequent post mortem determined that Harry's passing was caused by electrocution and not by the fall from a great height. I felt that Sarah, Harry's wife, derived little solace from the distinction.

There was a sequel to this sad tale which helped me decide I was once again in the wrong business. Sarah was naturally upset by this unexpected turn of events but when she was handed her late husband's belongings at the hospital, she was unable to find his wallet, and I had the impression this upset her even more. He'd been a scrap metal dealer, so he would have conducted his business transactions in cash. Sarah came to my coffee bar demanding to know if anyone, especially Charlie, had appeared to be rather more flush than usual:

"Has Charlie been flashing the cash?"

Not running a den of thieves, I offered an offended denial, but excused the emotion of her double loss.

Some weeks later, a couple of detectives turned up, knocking at the door as I was preparing to open up.

"Have you seen Charlie this morning?" they asked.

"Well, yes," I replied, "he came by an hour ago and asked if I would like half a pig! He said it was already dead and butchered, although I thought he didn't need to say that, as it was only half a pig he was offering. 'Don't want any money', he said. 'Just want to get rid of it quick, before it goes off.'"

"And did you oblige Charlie in his endeavour to dispose of this half a pig, sir?" the larger detective asked, slipping just a trace of a smile towards his colleague.

Policemen are noted for not allowing their innate sense of humour to interfere when making official enquiries, aren't they?

"Well, no," I replied, deadpan. "What would I do with half a pig? I don't use fresh meat here, just prepacked stuff, you know. Anyway, knowing Charlie, as I do, I gained the impression that he might well have come by this item," – I paused carefully – "in dubious circumstances."

"Quite right, sir, quite right." Detective number one was by now unable to conceal his amusement. "The slaughterhouse at Keighley was broken into last night and certain items, including the two halves of a pig, were unlawfully removed by, shall we say, person or persons unknown?"

"But we know, don't we, sir?" chipped in detective number two. "You and I know. Any idea where he might be now, sir?"

Not a clue.

I didn't see Charlie in the coffee bar for several months after that.

He did pop up again though, and even then, it was 'in dubious circumstances.'

I had a phone call early one morning from the cleaning lady to say someone had broken the lock on the door. When I got there, the police were already doing their stuff. All the machines had been broken into and all money taken. My clientele knew perfectly well on which day the collector came to clear the takings, so it was no surprise that this incident occurred on the night prior to his regular visit.

Of course, my clientele knew equally well who was responsible. They also knew all about the fifty-fifty split. Over the next couple of days, I explained loudly and clearly to anyone within earshot that, although the rental company undoubtedly had insurance to cover such incidents, no one had been prepared to insure me.

On the third day, he rose again. I received an intimation furtively delivered by one of the younger lads that, if I got in my car and parked at the back of the fire station at two o'clock, I would learn something to my advantage. Well, he didn't say that exactly.

Promptly at two o'clock, in broad daylight, Charlie came sauntering casually around the corner of the fire station. He was wearing a long fawn gabardine raincoat of the type favoured by a certain television detective of the era. Hands in pockets, shoulders hunched, he clutched the coat tightly around him. Without so much as a guilty glance over his shoulder to ensure we were unobserved, he opened the passenger door and slid into the seat. From within the folds of the raincoat, he lowered to the floor a bulging blue cotton bag of the type used by banks for transporting quantities of cash.

Still without looking at me, he calmly said, "We didn't know you wasn't insured. That's your 'alf."

Equally calmly, he opened the door, climbed out and walked off around the corner of the fire station.

I could hardly go to the police, could I?

That night, I closed the coffee bar – permanently.

I never saw Charlie again, although I did hear, later, that he and his two closest 'colleagues' had been detained …

At Her Majesty's Pleasure.

*

HOW TO SELL A PROPERTY NOBODY WANTS

Back at the guesthouse, also the family home, an interesting situation developed – scary at the time. Stony broke, with a bank balance in the mystical realms of negativity, as well as trying to find a job in environmental work, I was trying desperately to sell the property.

For several reasons, not least its isolation, as a business it was a failure. We had to sell.

It was a two-and-a-half-acre island in sweeping Brontëesque landscape sold off years earlier by the owner of the surrounding few thousand acres of steep, sheep-grazing, hiker-friendly, frequently rain soaked and wind blasted heather and rocks lost in a little-known part of the West Riding of Yorkshire termed descriptively, 'The Dales'. Its umbilical connection to the nearby village, euphemistically known thereabouts as 'civilisation', was a mile or so of narrow single-track tarmac that ended at our front door. By narrow I mean that when the furniture pantechnicon came to 'remove' us, its tyre walls were dangerously abraded by the rocks between which it perilously passed; the neighbouring farmer on his tractor, instead of using the road, reached the village by traversing the adjacent streamside meadows.

To the north, actual civilisation occurred in the elegantly civilised spa town of Harrogate. To the south and east sprawled the depressing agglomeration of desolate moors and industrial revolution that were Cleckhuddersfax (Cleckheaton, Huddersfield and Halifax), which included depressing Dewsbury with nearby Leeds, and Bradford. And between Bradford and Leeds was Slaithwaite, birthplace of Harold Wilson. A fact which vitally affects my story.

It was 1969. Harold Wilson was serving his first term as Labour Prime Minister. Bradford Corporation was controlled by Labour politicians and, I don't doubt, many of its employees would have been Party supporters. Textile mills and engineering works dominated the city skylines and the populace held strong socialist views.

By the time we arrived in the remotest part of the Dales, in the early 1960s, the surrounding acres had passed to David, the nephew of the man who'd sold 'our' island. David and his wife occupied the long, low farmhouse that lay not a hundred yards down the lane. In buying the twelve-bedroom cottage-guesthouse, we'd acquired a gentleman's agreement with David, to rent for a nominal sum first, a less than adequate water supply from a spring on his land and second, the use of a piece of land on the opposite side of the road for parking eight or ten cars. We assumed David would extend the same facilities to a buyer.

Wrong.

Despite the Estate Agent's considerable advertising, the only serious prospective purchaser was the Property Department of the City of Bradford Corporation, thirty miles away. Their interest was the potential for conversion to an outdoor-pursuits centre for underprivileged children and teenagers from their city. When visited by a Corporation official, I enthusiastically encouraged the idea. David was horrified at the prospect of his rural idyll being shattered by weekly arrivals of minibuses full of noisy youngsters who would have little or no idea of country life. In retrospect, Joyce and I would have sympathised but, at the time, survival was our principal concern – and survival meant selling.

David wrote letters and made phone calls to the Corporation officials concerned, pointing out that it would be irresponsible to bring young people into an area littered with the remains of old lead-mining shafts. There were a couple, but they'd been adequately filled in or fenced. Where the ghyll gurgling through our land ran onto his, there was a thirty-foot waterfall and, David again pointed out, accidents would happen. Therefore, he wouldn't extend the water and carparking agreements to them. He would thwart any possible sale to Bradford Corporation.

As to the water, the supply we took from David's spring was so poor that our paying guests were horrified when, if the two toilets serving the twelve bedrooms were flushed simultaneously, they had to wait a little while before continuing their ablutions.

The local Water Board had a pipeline running from somewhere upstream into a treatment plant on our rented car park. After mixing with chemicals, the water couldn't be used for human consumption until it had travelled a thousand yards down the pipeline towards the village. The cost of linking into that pipeline and bringing the supply back up to our cottage proved prohibitive but, with help from the officials in Bradford, I discovered we had a legal right to take water from the ghyll for domestic purposes.

It would need to be treated but again the Bradford people researched. There was a device available which, inserted into the extraction pipe and using a minimal electricity supply, would treat the water with ultra-violet light making it fit for humans.

Also, there was space on our land, adjacent to the road, to clear and level an area for several minibuses or cars. Great, we thought, we've cracked the problems.

David somehow heard this; he became abusive, upsetting the Bradford officials even more. On submitting proposals to their superiors, the officials were told they couldn't go ahead with the project unless there was adequate provision from the public water supply.

Stymied again!

Thinking he had us where he wanted us, David offered, through the estate agents, four thousand pounds to buy back the cottage and land. This was less than we'd paid for it four years earlier and little over half our asking price of six thousand five hundred pounds. To have accepted would have left us homeless with an overdraft.

When I told the Corporation official of David's attitude, he came to see me. He looked around the spotless but freezing sitting room, saw the kids playing outside, caught the worried look between Joyce, serving tea, and me. He smiled.

"That's not very nice of David. We've already set things in motion from our end. We've begun procedures applying for planning permission and putting advertisements in the local papers. Unless you can resolve the problem of the water supply it seems we can't purchase your property. But David won't know that. Why don't you tell him that unless he'll better our offer, you'll close the deal with the Corporation? See how much you can get out of him."

It's been put to me that this behaviour wasn't typical of an official employed by a City Corporation. I can only suggest that the socio-political background I sketched at the outset of this true tale could explain his sympathetic attitude. I was a little guy being squeezed by a comparatively wealthy gentleman – a member of the Conservative Party and the influential Country Landowners Association. Perhaps the head of the Property Department in Bradford Town Hall felt that my neighbour was using his position to take advantage of me.

Or perhaps he was a family man himself.

I instructed the Estate Agents accordingly. David increased his offer to seven thousand pounds. By this time I was frustrated and desperate. I insisted the agents to tell David that, if he wanted to keep us from selling to the Corporation, it would cost him ten thousand pounds.

David responded with an offer of nine.

I replied, "Eleven thousand plus all our fees and expenses and signed by the weekend, or else …!"

The agents were horrified. My solicitor was horrified. Joyce was horrified.

They all threw up their hands and warned me against it, but what did I have to lose? I didn't sleep well that night. Next day, Friday, the agent called me.

"David has signed."

I accept that my negotiations might have been unethical but, sometimes, if one is bitten, one has to bite back. We had a respite from our financial worries. We could pay off the bank and have a few thousand pounds in hand with which to re-establish our lives elsewhere.

Nine months later, after we'd moved to Cornwall, came Christmas. In the post, a greetings card from …

David.

*

FISH 'N' CHIPS

I was back home with two bankrupt businesses to my name: a licensed restaurant and a licensed guesthouse; as well as a wife and three children under the age of ten. What do we do when we're in trouble? If we're smart, we pray. I'd abandoned church worship years earlier, but I hadn't lost my trust in God's goodness.

"OK God, where am I going wrong? It's not for want of trying. What the heck do I do now?" is more or less what I said to Him.

In true Biblical fashion – Lo! It came to pass!

Among the last of the faithful few customers of my now defunct licensed restaurant, was a retired Lieutenant Colonel of the Black Watch Regiment. In his mid-sixties and bored, he'd bought a bankrupt fish and chip shop a few miles up the road. With military efficiency, he'd got it up and running and it was so prosperous that he was a good spender on his day off, when he brought his wife to my restaurant.

When I realised I was going to have to close down, I, the bankrupt ex-corporal, said to the prosperous retired Colonel:

"Bill (after a couple of brandies, of course we were on first-name terms), Bill, if I came to work for you, for just a couple of weeks, for no pay, would you show me the basics of the business? Then, if you think I could cope with it, I'll go and find a run-down shop somewhere and see if I can do what you've done."

And the Colonel said to the bankrupt:

"Joseph, if you come and work for me you'll b****y well do as you're told and you'll b****y well get paid."

I duly attended at his chip shop and studied the secrets of his success:

After about six weeks, Bill said one day:

"Wyn and I haven't had a holiday for a couple of years so, now you know how to run the place, you know the customers, you know the suppliers, we'll leave you to it. Take twenty quid a week for yourself, put twenty quid a week in the bank to pay the bills and send the rest in an envelope (yes, seriously!) to my daughter in Ringwood. Open when you like over Christmas and New Year and I'll be in touch."

This was early in November 1968.

After that, Bill and Wyn never did return to the shop.

Three months later… In February '69 came his first phone call. From France.

"There's a chap coming to see you on Tuesday. Take stock, get his cheque to that value and give him the keys. I've sold up. If you haven't already emptied the drinks cupboard, just help yourself before he comes and I'll be in touch."

I know what you're thinking, and yes, I did hear from him again, soon after that.

"I'm negotiating to buy a business in Guernsey and I'd like you to relocate your family and go into partnership with me."

Joyce and I got excited. But then Bill discovered that, because he was a non-native of the island, he would have to pay substantial taxes up front.

Next thing I knew, he was back in England and had bought a closed-down chip shop in Devizes, Wiltshire.

"If you still have your van (I did), go to Leeds and buy (so much) fish and (so much) wrapping paper and come straight down here. We'll open this one together for Easter. I've booked you a room at the pub across the road."

When I arrived at said pub I had a pleasant surprise.

There was a chap sitting in the bar when I went in. Strumming a guitar, as chaps often did in the '60s. I had no idea who he was, but he was practising a song. He asked if I liked it.

"Yes," I said, "I do like that song."

He released it later that year, on an album. Then in 1974 as a single.

Streets of London. Remember Ralph McTell?

Bill and I opened for Easter. We did a roaring trade for a couple of weeks. Bill was delighted and paid me well for my trouble.

*

By now, he had taught me all I desired to know about the business and in working alongside him I had gained all the confidence I needed – together Joyce and I could do it, if we could find the right place.

First, disposal of the assets in Yorkshire. And that is a story in itself.

(See HOW TO SELL A PROPERTY NOBODY WANTS in this anthology)

Second, find the right place for our next move. Specialist Estate/Business Agencies, phone calls, miles of motoring to view possibilities; and, after a few weeks, it paid off.

In St Columb Major, a small inland town on the A39 main road between Bodmin and the north Cornwall coast, I found a High Street grocery business with a fish-and-chip café and takeaway hidden at the back. Being pretty well bankrupt due to family difficulties and illness, the owner was asking a reasonable price.

I explained to the local bank manager (later to become a customer) he'd be failing in his duty to the community, as well as the functional obligation incumbent on his position within the financial and social fabric of the town, to lubricate the wheels of local commerce, if he didn't facilitate my acquisition and revitalisation of this failing business. Of course, he saw my point and obliged with appropriate financial assistance.

After closing the grocery business, we made suitable modifications to the building and equipment, and with the family settled in, we had two satisfactory seasons in our Cornish Chippy.

In **November 1973** we leased the business to an Italian family.

In **October 2019,** (I'm now living in a nursing home in Wales) a friend brought me some holiday snaps just taken, of that Cornish Chippy – still, forty-six years on, with our name on the fascia board and descendants of the same family running it.

I mentioned two satisfactory seasons but we'd come to the conclusion we'd prefer a more active and lucrative location. After two and a half years of jolly hard work – as well as some play – we sold the business on a twenty-one-year's lease (later converted to freehold). We paid off the bank two and a half years into a fifteen-year agreed term and set about looking for a better possibility.

From Penzance in Cornwall to Camberley in Surrey, I searched for a suitable place on the A30, the road that carried the London and Home Counties holiday traffic to the West Country. All the really good sites had, by the early 1970s, been snapped up by the catering groups and fast food chains. We couldn't compete in that section of the commercial property market.

Back to the Agencies. In the course of a series of viewings, from Durham to Norwich to Anglesey, I found myself in Llanrhaeadr-ym-Mochnant. This small community lying close to the famous Pistyll Rhaeadr, highest waterfall in Wales, is set in the enchanting beauty of the Berwyn Mountains. Since my conversation with God in Yorkshire and our subsequent change of fortune, I had learned to follow hunches, to listen to a sort of voice-in-the-head that had brought me to surprisingly serendipitous situations. This was one such. (There were many more, if you care to find them in my other publications)

Clearly this was not to be considered as a chippy-favourable location, so why had I come by this route? Why this village? I parked, crossed the street and popped into the local branch of Midland Bank thinking to pick up a bit of local colour. Joyce had been heard to remark that I must've had some deep spiritual affinity with bank managers. It was another one who, now, would introduce us to what would prove to be our most successful business venture.

After the customary conversational pleasantries with the manager, I raised the matter of finding … "Well look you, now," he said, "if you're interested in something like that, I know of a truly excellent proposition. Three hours down the coast of Cardigan Bay it is, see. A café and takeaway. Closed due to family problems. Bankrupt and in the hands of the Official Receiver. In a filthy condition but in my professional opinion, it has the potential you're looking for. It is mainly seasonal, but there should be some winter trade."

Serendipity, see?

He made a couple of phone calls, arranged for us to pick up the keys from the agents and off we went again. The High Street location, in Tywyn, Gwynedd, a few hundred yards from the seafront, looked right; the property seemed sound; the condition was filthier than the bank manager had described.

We looked at each other and said, "OK. LET'S DO IT."

So grateful were we, we would've liked to have given our overdraft to that Midland Bank manager but we were banking with Barclays. Joyce insisted I must have once again discovered some mystical affinity with the local manager. This time, the five-figure loan was, by far, our biggest yet. More confident than ever before, we launched ourselves into the final and most successful chapter of our joint business career.

We didn't see the clouds on the horizon.

With the three children, now aged thirteen, eleven and six, crammed into the back seat of our big old Rover, we set off for the long haul north from Cornwall into Wales.

Our route took us across Bodmin Moor, past the historical Jamaica Inn, famously in Daphne du Maurier's novel of that name. The first of the winter's snow had begun to powder the landscape and even to lie on the road. Although we quickly emerged from that fall, we could see it following us as we turned towards Bristol and, by the time we crossed the Severn Bridge, it was fully dark. And still the snow fell.

I'd already planned the route across Wales, but map reading and finding bilingual signposts in a strange, sparsely populated country, at night, in a snowstorm, was a first for us all.

Our speed was reduced accordingly and in the wee small hours, with only about twenty-five miles left to go, we came across a turning with a sign in the headlights: 'MACHYNLLETH'. And underneath, 'Via Narrow Mountain Road'. Ominous to say the least, but we'd left the last town ten miles behind. After a brief debate, we decided to go for it.

In the succeeding half-century, we've used that twenty miles of rising, falling, winding road hundreds of times, usually in daylight but never again in heavy snow. Without a doubt, we rate it one of the most beautiful scenic drives in the whole of Britain; especially if there is a light powdering of snow. It provides magnificent landscapes and lakescapes in the Plynlimon mountain range but, on that particular winter's night, we saw nothing that was not illuminated by our own headlights.

Around four in the morning, we topped a brow and began the five-mile descent towards Machynlleth. Owain Glyndŵr, one of Wales' most famous sons, was crowned Prince of Wales here in 1404 and he established his parliament in the town. It's in the valley of the river Dyfi and fourteen miles from our destination.

Already in lowest gear and creeping gently forward, we saw in the headlights a car that had left the road and was perched at an angle on the low bank. A man was walking towards us, waving his arms. Gingerly, I touched the brakes and we slithered into the bank just yards from the other car. It was on the edge of a frighteningly steep unfenced slope that plunged away hundreds of feet into the eerily lit semi-darkness of the snow-covered valley.

The driver and his companion, who lived in the valley, spoke English with an accent that indicated, clearly, their mother-tongue. Politely but firmly, they suggested it might be unwise to continue down the hill. After one look over the edge, I was not inclined to argue the point. Obviously, no one was going any further before dawn at the earliest and, glad we'd packed lots of blankets in the car, we resigned ourselves to the inevitable and wrapped up as well as we could, hopefully to get a few hours' sleep.

The three children seemed unfazed and soon settled down. After all, they were on another adventure with Mum and Dad. Naturally, the temperature in the car quickly began to drop and I ran the engine from time to time rather than let it get too cold for comfort. Without a thermometer we had no way of knowing the outside temperature but in the morning the snow had a certain cr-r-runch to it.

It was around eight o'clock, when daylight revealed the awesome beauty around us, that we gained some inkling of the scenic pleasures our new home held in store for us. It was only then we realised how close we'd come to disaster.

We eventually got both cars on the road again and made our way the few hundred yards further down to where, unbelievably, there was almost no snow and very little ice.

*

On 1st December 1973 we took possession of our new home. There was a striking contrast between the idyllic location – on the coast of Cardigan Bay, within sight of Cadair Idris – and the debris of a bankrupt business. Horrendous, sickening even! Strewn about, lurking in almost inaccessible places were items normally to be expected in a garbage bin. No, I'm being unfair to garbage – the contents of those ominous grey boxes in public conveniences that are emptied by 'technicians' in HAZMAT suits. Judging by the litter of half-burnt candles, joss sticks and sundry sanitary paraphernalia, the previous occupants had departed in a toxic, drug-fuelled despair, carelessly leaving the objectionable evidence of their inadequacy and failure behind them. Is that gratuitously judgemental? I've tried to make it objective.

Again, we went through the routine of planning permissions (there's a separate story there, it took us twelve years to get the planners off our backs), building alterations, complete re-equipping including a five-ton freezer in the cellar and a ruinously expensive, stainless steel frying range. (I did say, a few pages back, it was our biggest bank loan ever.)

My earlier experiences with Colonel Bill, followed by our own two seasons in Cornwall, ensured we had everything in place. The five-ton freezer. The range. Three tons of potatoes in the 'prep' room. Gallons (soon to be litres) of frying oil. And a stack of wrapping paper. (The use of traditional newspaper had been banned only recently when it was found that urine from the mice that frequently nested in it, had been responsible for a number of cases of ill-health in human eaters of fish 'n' chips). Our own children and some of their schoolmates on parade each morning. Joyce, now familiar with the drill, helped our first ten days run with military precision. From the minute we opened the doors on that first Thursday, the smell of the hot pans, the unique sizzle of frying chips, the inescapable, unmistakable aroma of vinegar on hot battered cod, told the story. By this time, we were all old hands.

We'd got the show on the road.

And the local people, Welsh and English alike, welcomed us.

Speaking of language, within the first week of opening, I reprimanded several in the late-night queues for using certain words and phrases apparently common to both English and Welsh.

"My wife and my children never hear bad language in our home and anyone using it will not be served. Your choice. Good behaviour or no supper."

Cloud of angels they were, after that.

There was another 'chippy' at the other end of town. I occasionally heard reports of fighting and similar boisterous behaviour involving broken windows and other damage.

Not in my chippy. Not my angels. Over thirty-five years on, as family men and women, they'd still greet me in the street as I went shopping on my mobility scooter.

After that first crazy Bank Holiday period, there was a short lull before the main holiday season began in earnest. By October, when historically, we were told, the visitors would be gone, all the family were ready for the half-term break. Not only some respite from the daily pressures of coping with a wholly unexpected volume of business, but also time to take stock of our lives – and consider how each of the family would be affected by this remarkable change in our fortunes. Would it – could it – last?

Our maximum count came in the early 1980s, when, during the summer months, we frequently served up to eight hundred meals between noon and around midnight.

In trying to analyse the basis of our success, I later concluded that, apart from the fact that we served appetising food, including truly excellent chips, there was an underlying factor that, initially, had escaped us.

Pre-purchase research had revealed there were many holiday homes on this section of the coast, especially several thousand static caravans within a ten to fifteen-mile semi-circle. Semi-circle only, because the other half of the circle was the waters of Cardigan Bay. Which is what attracted them all in the first place!

It was still the era when different areas and their associated industries each closed separately for their annual two weeks holiday, thus enabling our 'season' to extend over some eight to ten weeks of peak trade.

The static 'vans were mainly used by families who derived their living from the motor manufacturing industry and its allied trades in the industrial Midlands, a little over two hours away to the east.

During the mid- to late-seventies and early eighties, the car makers, along with other industrial sectors, declined rapidly, resulting in thousands of redundancies. Redundancy money – severance pay today – was The Word. Get it and spend it, then draw the dole. So they came to their holiday hideaways on the coast. But now it wasn't just their summer hols and weekends; it was for weeks at a time. Families appeared in our doorway two and even three times a day for us to feed them. (Our menus went far beyond the basic fish 'n' chips.) And we did, gladly. Tongue in cheek, we said that their misfortune was making our fortune.

And so it went on for twelve years, at the end of which my spine decided enough was enough. (But that's another story, not in this collection, but in the full-length memoir we wrote together and available on Kindle, *A MARRIAGE*)

I don't recall all the figures; I only know that our opening week's trade far exceeded what Bill and I had done in his first week in the Devizes shop. As I write this, over forty years later, the only statistic that remains with me is that, in twelve half-years of trading, we fried over 500 tons of potatoes.

By the mid-1970s, things had changed more than somewhat. Even with winter closure imposed on us by the town planners, our turnover/profit ratio soon put our earnings (briefly) into Maggie Thatcher's top tax band. In two years, we'd gone from paying minimal tax to 90 pence in the pound!

Our five-figure loan, on which the bank manager had agreed a ten-year term, was paid off by the end of our second season. That bank manager, clearly, Joyce insisted, forevermore under my spell, eagerly offered further finance should we wish to acquire additional premises or otherwise expand. He acknowledged, perhaps indiscreetly, that ours was the second most lucrative business in the town. Discretion precludes disclosure of the most lucrative. It was from the shop next door that I obtained our annual supply of whole sirloins of Welsh Black beef, subsequently served with the most deliciously flavoursome and aromatic chips …

Our ship had come in. Never again would we have to lie awake worrying about paying the bills, clothing our children, or making tough decisions about uprooting them and moving on. We were home at last. Our last, final, permanent, home.

*

Our greatest success was our chips.

It's no secret. There are certain known factors which, I hasten to repeat, I had learned in my few weeks alongside Colonel Bill in his Yorkshire shop.

The potato:

Maris Piper and Wilja were the two main crop varieties most favoured in the trade to produce crisp, dry chips.

Preparation:

The potatoes were peeled in a machine known as a 'rumbler'. Electrically operated, it tumbled the potatoes around in a drum with an abrasive lining. When peeled, the potatoes were immediately chipped by an electric chipper before being transferred into sixteen-gallon plastic tubs. There they stood in a solution of water and a powder or liquid additive known as 'dry-white'.

After some hours of soaking, the solution was drained off and the chips dried white. Without the additive, they dried dark grey to black, just as they do at home.

The frying medium:

In the couple of centuries prior to my learning the trade, the most widely used medium seems to have been beef dripping. Following Colonel Bill's lead, in my couple of seasons in Cornwall, I too used it. However, in all aspects of the food industry, from abattoir and poultry packer to greasy spoon and Michelin starred restaurant, Food Hygiene was the new buzz word.

I no longer recall the details of why (probably health and hygiene) dripping was rapidly phased out and replaced by a variety of vegetable oils including rapeseed, sunflower and palm oil (pity the poor rainforests!) After moving to Wales, I, like many another at the time, tried about eight of the products on offer. I quickly settled on one. A blend of several oils, it was sold under the trade name FRYTOL. In order to be certain of my supply, I bought about £3,000 worth at the beginning of each season and had it delivered on demand by the supplier. Having settled on that one product, I used it until I sold up twelve years later. Thereafter, we used it at home in our domestic fryer for perhaps ten years, until it disappeared from the market. Apart from its suitability for purpose, it possessed one other, most important, attribute – it did not leave a heavy, sticky layer on the stainless steel and other work surfaces. This reduced substantially the time and effort required to keep everything clean. Clearly, my predecessors had never discovered this product.

Blanching:

This means simply part-frying the chips, at 120°F, until they begin to soften but without showing any change of colour. This took about three minutes. After draining, the chips were transferred into eight-gallon plastic tubs and left to cool.

Finishing:

To finish cooking the chips, I raised the temperature of the oil to 190°F and cooked until suitably crisp and brown, again about three to four minutes. This was done only in the minutes immediately prior to being sold in the take-away or served to the restaurant.

In the words of my old geometry master – Q.E.D.

Blanching and finishing is the method used to this day by our children in their domestic kitchens.

After some thirty-five years of retirement, since I eat only home-made, I have no idea whether any of today's commercial fryers and catering chefs follow my practices but, judging by comments from friends and acquaintances, I guess probably not many. Shame. I understand frozen chips are more in vogue these days. No wonder people complain.

It was a few years after we had sold up that we realised our good fortune had come at a price. It was a price we willingly paid, as the accumulated funds financed our world-wide travel over the next thirty years – and that really is ANOTHER STORY.

Forty-one years later, at the end of June 2015,

at the highest point on the road where we had spent that snowy night in 1973,

a road we used a few hundred times over the years,

along with our three children Lesley, Adrian, Craig and his wife Pamela,

I scattered Joyce's ashes in the wind.

*

No Time to Rest

The days grow long as I grow old.

As more and more I feel the cold,

Creaking back and aching knee,

In silent chorus telling me,

Old man, you need to rest.

No more I stride across the hills

By babbling burns and gurgling ghylls;

Purple heather, yellow gorse,

By Malham's Cove and Aire's sweet source.

With never time to rest.

I miss wild Rombald's heathered moor.

Nor e'er again, from my front door,

To gaze across to Otley Chevin.

It seemed we lived quite near to heaven.

Who needs to take a rest?

'Cross Dartmoor, Exmoor, Bodmin too,

I've worn out many a walking shoe.

And, at the old Jamaica Inn,

Watched misty evening drawing in.

And there we took a rest.

The baying hounds, the huntsman's horse;

They take a life without remorse.

Yet farmer's poultry, shepherd's lamb,

Brer fox will kill, nor give a damn.

He never stops to rest.

Back then, in Cornish coombes and bays,

Wiled we away long summer days.

While, further south, they'd mine the clay.

And copper ore and tin assay.

Sometimes we took a rest.

From Knockan Crag, to reach Stac Pollaidh,

'Cross peaty bog, climb sandstone solid.

Climbing to Torridon's craggy peaks.

Likely too, you'll snag your breeks.

'Twill soon be time to rest

Pausing high in Torridon's corries,

Far from the roar of M1's lorries;

Body aching, racked with pain,

I'll never climb Beinn Eighe again.

I think I'll take a rest.

By Cwm Pennant lies Tanat Vale.

According to the minstrel's tale,

The sweet Melangell came to pray.

Nor e'er felt need to go away.

Perhaps 'tis there I'll rest.

Where Severn rises 'mong the peat,

Where curlew calls and spring lambs bleat,

Nor any place, from pole to pole,

Cast such a spell upon my soul.

I feel the need to rest.

Then old Alzheimer cast his spell.

Across our lives dark shadows fell.

My true love's mind, aye seeped away.

And ne'er again I'll hear her say,

Why don't we take a rest?

Glyndwr's Way we'd oft times tread.

My true love's ashes there are spread.

I feel her presence as I pass.

I'll meet again my Yorkshire lass,

When I go to my rest.

*

QUINACRIDONE PIGMENTS: DO THEY WARRANT THEIR ELEVATED STATUS IN MODERN ART?

I never went to Art School. Actually, I didn't go to school at all. Not that I'm illiterate or ignorant of the arts, or unaware of the finer nuances of civilised experiential existence (in which I include Epicureanism). I recall with nostalgic regret that in the remote Pyrenean community into which I was born, between Segre and the Franco-Spanish-Andorran border confluence, no-one had heard of the Guinness Book of Records.

From infancy to early adulthood I herded the village's several hundred goats in the traditional way of my forbears, whose knowledge and wisdom filtered through to me and my very few peers in the manner of any such close-knit, isolated community. As long as I wielded my slingshot adequately in deterrence of any rare marauding wolf or lynx and similarly protected the new-born kids from the attentions of the many griffon vultures as they eyed us from neighbouring crags or circled menacingly overhead, I was left to my own devices.

Marginally more formal education I derived from intermittent meetings with the visiting Catholic priest who, I should add, was the first to recognise and foster my inherent skill with charcoal stick on paper. When I say 'stick' I do not, of course, refer to the product available in a sophisticated Artists' Supplies Store; rather to lumps of partially combusted wood remnant in the ashes of my occasional fire on a neighbouring hillside…you understand. The border authorities of all three neighbouring nations were inclined to turn a blind eye to the ostensibly peripatetic perambulations of these itinerant clerics. Of course, everyone else knew it was frequently commodities other than communion wine that accompanied them from community to community.

Thus was I deprived of an early opportunity to achieve fame and acclaim. The outside world never learned of my ability, at the tender age of seven, with eyes closed and nostrils flaring, olfactorily to differentiate between a Spanish Brandy and a Napoleon Cognac. Heaven forbid I should ever experience an event disabling the olfactory cortex of my brain and inducing permanent, total anosmia. Taste and smell are so closely related within the brain's processes that such an occurrence would have rendered me unable ever again to experience the exquisite joy of an expertly distilled, aged and blended Napoleon. Strangely, that couple of decades in which I spent almost every hour, waking and sleeping, in close proximity to hundreds of highly malodourous Caprinae did not adversely influence my seriously sensitive olfactory function. Born and brought up with it, I was rarely aware of it.

It was not until I reached my thirteenth birthday that I was formally introduced to the delight of imbibing the divine intoxicant while consigning the Spanish product I mentioned earlier to the stables for cleaning purposes. Later, I learned to savour the exquisitely smooth, rich aromas and nuances of related Gallic genius. At the same time, I and my peers were rigorously indoctrinated into (and cautioned against) the powerful inebriant qualities of such spirituous delights though there were, regrettably, many whose failure to heed the warning led to an early grave.

I should add that my introduction to many of life's mysteries and the broadening of my academic knowledge, not to mention linguistic gymnastics, I owe to the mysterious appearance among us of an English Benedictine scholar who, for some reason he never disclosed had felt the need to distance himself from his monastic community near the Rhône Delta on France's Mediterranean coast. One is, of course, aware that the monastic rule founded by St Benedict around the sixth century AD included lay brothers and later, nuns whose patroness, St Scholastica, was his sister. It is also a matter of record that the era of Benedictine preponderance ended around the middle of the 12th century, after which Benedictine monasticism declined into decadence over the next three centuries. So perhaps neither man nor woman is immune. But who am I to pontificate? I digress, a fault to which I am given, alas…

Among the multifarious matters to which this erudite intellectual drew my attention was the liqueur that famously bears the escutcheon of his religious order. Certainly, I found this a pleasant enough sensual experience and we would occasionally end an evening of esoteric and abstruse study with a small measure, before he would take himself off to his place of residence somewhere in the cave system close to which our village lay; and I to my caprine compound, accompanied only by my faithful Pyrenean mountain dog, Pablo.

I confess, eventually I found his constant eulogising of its virtues and merits irksome. Of course, I could never agree with his declaration of the superiority of the cloying, over-sweet and herb-perfumed liqueur in comparison to the exquisite experience of an expertly distilled, aged and blended Napoleon Cognac (marginally chilled.)

In his defence, it was from this scholarly Epicurean that I learned the practice of allowing the brandy, as it slowly warms to blood heat thereby releasing its unique characteristic essence, to lingeringly stimulate the receptor cells located on the taste buds along the sides of the tongue, then lingually coaxing it gently towards the epiglottis and eventually, progressively into the oesophagus. Surely one of life's unsurpassable, extreme enchantments. Of course, the receptors and taste buds terminate prior to the tonsilatory and epiglottal areas so that, although there is an enjoyable residual aftertaste, (the 'finish' so beloved of oenophiles) the oesophagus and stomach fail completely to deliver any prolongation of the experience; there is, however, a comforting warmth induced (internally of course) in the abdominal region. I confess to wondering whether or not his sheer delight and enthusiasm for the subject, clearly manifest on his beaming visage, conflicted to some degree with the spirit of his order (no witticism intended though, I admit, accomplished).

Today, through the freedom of movement and trade within the greater community of the European Union, all citizens of that great twentieth century institution can be introduced to the product of such expertise at the youngest possible age. Unfortunately, in this era of ultimate globalisation, inhabitants of more recently civilised lands far away in the occident and the orient have also been introduced to the delights of the epicurean hedonism derived from their European cradle, thus creating a demand that, following the rubrics of Keynesian economics, has influenced adversely the market's demand for, and cost of, the product.

Years passed and the advent of the infamous Spanish dictatorship brought considerable localised changes. I was recruited by guerrilla co-villagers as my pastoral lifestyle was well suited to monitoring the various nefarious pedestrian and mule-born traffic over less accessible routes across the rugged Pyrenean terrain. I recall how colleagues would attract the attention of their adversaries by flashing torches and luring them on as Pablo and I guided them into more and more inaccessible places, then abandoning them to their own devices while we returned to our village to celebrate. (A practice, I later learned, reminiscent of the activities of a British group known, historically, as the Cornish Wreckers.)

Our activities aggravated the authorities somewhat, until Franco's ruthless regime forced our whole village to desert the idyllic rustic lifestyle and move from our remote mountain paradise to a more populous area where we could easily be controlled – it happened throughout many regions of the Provinces of Catalonia, Aragon and Navarra. I left Pablo to shepherd the wild goats alone.

*

A year or two after the demise of the Generalissimo, a matter the cause of which remains hotly disputed in my homeland, I returned to the mountains with my Welsh wife. In several of the more isolated ruined villages we found remains of military artefacts – mortar shell cases, for example – some of which now grace our home in Wales as gruesome souvenirs of the irreversibly inconsolable heartbreak of the Catalan nation to which I belong. I note there is strong support for National Independence for the Catalan Nation – but I am too old …

This return visit occurred prior to the opening of international borders within Europe. Limitation of currency movement and production of passports at the crossing points were still rigidly enforced. So too was restriction on the passage of tobacco products and spirituous commodities (including Napoleon Cognac). However, it so happened that during the 1970s and 80s (our early tourism period) on one of our scores of crossings, in both directions, of the high Pyrenean passes, I was driving our Land Rover Santana 4 x 4 Camper Conversion. Our itinerary took us by way of one of the more remote and less frequented routes I had used in my youthful clandestine activities during the dictatorship. I cannot flatter it with the term 'road'; it tested the robustness of my spine as much as the sturdiness of the vehicle. I recall it was in Basque country near Larrun, a minor mountain peak. For many miles we saw no indication of a border checkpoint nor any sign of human life, but we most certainly started the day in Spain and ended it in France without anyone of either nationality demanding sight of our passports. I did not shout my discovery from the rooftops; rather I made use of it on numerous occasions thereafter, so enhancing considerably my ability to enjoy, and assist others in their enjoyment of, an already somewhat hedonistic taste for life's pleasures among which I acknowledge a mild bibulous tendency though, I must insist, never libidinous.

*

The compulsory relocation of our village community had brought us to the sea, to Barcelona where, for a few years among our neighbours was one Pablo Picasso, a person of some fame as a painter and, later, other forms of the visual arts. It was my association with this iconic character that awakened my interest in more civilised aspects of life and introduced me to the enchantments of Epicurean philosophy – not to mention renewal of my acquaintance with a renowned product of the Cognac region of Western France. The uniquely intimate topographical knowledge acquired in my youth now facilitated the import of this commodity in adequate measure.

Perhaps slightly more obscure than matters spirituous, though, in my opinion, of equal importance, is a proficiency in differentiating between the many and varied fragrances and perfumes to be encountered when awakening in the gentle early morning light of an unfamiliar boudoir. This latter expertise in olfactory perception has, on more than one occasion, saved me from an embarrassedly mumbled, "Donde esto? Where am I?", the indiscreet utterance of which had, on an earlier excursion in the company of my randy Barcelona neighbour, resulted in permanent exclusion from the metamorphosis from 'unfamiliar' to 'familiar' in that particular boudoir (a progression devoutly to be wished – [or not, as the case may be.])

Living in close proximity to such blossoming artistic genius, I became fascinated by aspects of his talent and lifestyle. Which is why I mentioned Art School in the first place. Ask any painter who has progressed beyond struggling initiation into the basics of the discipline and you will learn that greatest among his complex of practical problems lies the mixing of various pigmental shades and textures, not to mention incompatible chemical constituents.

Achievement of precisely the desired conceptual effect – simulation of the tonal characteristics visually encountered in a momentary hallucination (howsoever induced) – mixing on the palette of a colour able to record permanently a fleeting, intangible, even abstract experience; such are the ultimate frustrations of any artist, while, at the same time, constituting the essential esoteric formula for success.

Which is why, when quinacridones, with their intense fluorescence, their disinclination to manageable gallimaufry and, to me, nasally irritant characteristics (have you ever taken a good whiff of your computer's printing ink?) appeared in 1958, I grudgingly and ungraciously acknowledged defeat. I gave up even on Cubism and, in a rare, atypical fit of pique, threw the lot at the canvas and, to my great surprise, found myself in the ranks of famed abstract impressionists. Hence my place, today, alongside Jackson Pollock and de Kooning, in the more discerning galleries and exhibitions of that persuasion.

*

SEYCHELLES SAILING

The following is an excerpt from some memoirs that my late wife and I put together after our world travels came to an end in 2011.

Joseph.

In November, '87 we flew to the Seychelles and went sailing on the Indian Ocean.

The End.

Joyce.

Don't take any notice of him. Reticence is one of Joseph's most endearing characteristics but he is more than usually uncommunicative about this particular excursion.

It's not his fault he's susceptible to mal-de-mer.

On one of our weekly visits to the local swimming pool, Edna, an occasional bird-watching companion, said casually while treading water at the deep end;

"Joyce, I've booked a berth on a seventeen-metre ketch lying in Mahé, Seychelles. We'll be sailing around those stunningly beautiful islands for three weeks, bird-watching – and it is fabulous bird-watching! Departure date's only two weeks away. If you're interested there's still a double-berth cabin available and you might get a discount if you book right away."

Joseph's expression as he abruptly turned and swam away was not encouraging, a fact Edna did not fail to notice.

She added conspiratorially, "I'm afraid they'll cancel the trip if no-one books that cabin. Can't you persuade him?"

She'd easily persuaded me so I exercised my feminine charms. A couple of weeks later, we flew to Nairobi where we took a small island-hopper plane to Mahé.

Picturesque, as any harbour will be in warm, tropical sunshine, the scene seemed set for a great adventure. Yachts, dinghies and power-boats jostled comfortably as the lightest of breezes rippled the waters of the marina. All six of us were, I thought, in great spirits as we gathered to go aboard.

From the jetty Joseph contemplated the ketch. Never one for premonitions, he complained in his most doom-laden voice, "I have a feeling this was not a good idea. I wanna to go home."

I squeezed his arm encouragingly as we went aboard.

We discovered that there are double-berth cabins, as on cruise ships and ferries, and then there are double-berth cabins, as at the sharp end of a seventeen-metre ketch. Surveying the cramped space and the bed where we were to sleep for the next three weeks, Joseph grumbled that his nose had already detected a skimming of diesel in the bilges. I didn't know what a bilge was.

"Don't be silly, take a pill or three and you'll enjoy it as much as I will," I laughingly joked.

I later regretted that remark.

Happily, Joseph's pills proved partially effective as we sailed southwest to visit the atoll island groups of Aldabra and Cosmoledo, many nautical miles away. I didn't know that miles at sea are different from miles on land. Not that it was significant; just another detail that distinguishes seafarers from landlubbers.

Our itinerary included the Comoros Islands, even further southwest towards Madagascar and Mozambique. Just the sound of these foreign names was romantic, as in 'Sinbad' and 'Marco Polo' and 'fabled shores.' I thrilled with the anticipation of adventure. At first.

"Comoros. Madagascar. Mozambique. C'mon Joe."

I call him Joe when he is in a bad mood. You might have thought it would upset him more but usually it did just the opposite.

"Remember we nearly bought a boat a couple of years ago, but you got all grumpy and said you can't trust boats and the sea and all that. Now you'll really find out what we've been missing. You'll see," I said, smiling encouragingly with all my teeth, "this is going to be some trip." His unchanging expression confirmed his unease.

Joseph.

A few days after leaving Mahé in quite calm conditions, things began to change. For the worse. Mechanical unreliability cast an ominous shadow among the already cloudy haze on the horizon. Indeed, as any seafarer worth his salt, or country boy cognisant with the behaviour of rooks and crows would have known, that very haze was portent enough.

We half dozen paying passengers commented that, because there was insufficient wind, the auxiliary engine had been called upon increasingly to maintain our seriously slow progress. Unusual bumps and shudders from beneath our feet brought puzzled frowns to the faces of our group. Their wind- and weather-beaten countenances didn't conceal the frowns of our captain and his two crewmen. Frowns more worried than puzzled. Experienced sailors that they were, uncaring they carried us, a group of innocent landlubbers, forward across this wide and dangerous ocean towards … who knew what perils of the deep lay ahead? Three whole bloody weeks!

Joyce.

Joseph was quieter even than usual.

About day six, after a number of these rumbled warnings, the engines stopped.

Joseph corrected me, "Engine! Only one."

No power. No wind. We stopped. No, that's not quite true. I thought one of the crew said we'd lost our way, but Joseph, still ominously subdued, corrected me again.

"It's a nautical term. The captain said we have 'lost weigh' meaning we are slowing down and will, quite soon, stop moving – correction, cease making forward progress."

He did not swell with supercilious pride in expounding this superior seafaring snippet. Anticipation of what would almost inevitably follow seemed to have induced a gloom even deeper than that he'd displayed on the jetty.

There was another movement that hadn't stopped. Joseph's despondency discernibly deepened. They put up a little sail at the front, in order to 'keep her head to the wind' or something.

Joseph, always concerned for my comfort, explained.

"Theoretically, this will reduce the violence of the pitching and rolling motion caused by the waves that keep hitting the sides with that uniquely irritating, slapping sound. Bloody nonsense."

He doesn't usually talk like that. I really don't think it made much difference. I learned a lot about sailing on this trip. Joseph, never of swarthy complexion, had turned several shades paler, before…well…perhaps I'll not bring that up.

Much more to the point was, why had weigh been lost?

Leading our expedition was Tony, a professional ornithologist, wildlife warden and tour guide, to whom we turned for information.

"It's something to do with a shaft which transmits power from the diesel engine to the propeller under the back of the boat. Mountings holding the shaft in place have somehow broken which in turn has damaged a part of the engine. They'll have to order a replacement part from Mahé, but they can't as we're out of range on the radio-telephone."

Joseph.

No engine? No electricity to operate the fridge-freezer? In the climate prevailing in that latitude? The dozen or more chickens, destined for dinner at intervals throughout the next couple of weeks, were soon pronounced no longer fit for human consumption.

Bare heads bowed, we lined the rail to witness the committal ceremony, as the foul-smelling fowls were chucked overboard. No doubt denizens of the deep welcomed a free lunch.

Joyce.

Joseph didn't visibly weep but the depth of his despair, contrasted to the eager expectant ethos prevalent among some of us prior to departure, was moving.

"There is," resumed our guide, conversationally, "an island not far away, where they can discreetly kill a turtle. This is illegal under conservation law but if they don't, we'll all be without dinner for days. They've put out a couple of hand lines to catch red snapper for dinner. As there's not much fresh water on board, it'll be necessary to drink wine with the red snapper. Also, everyone will have to make do with just one glass of water each per day – to wash your face and clean your teeth, at least until we reach land where, they say, we can get more."

Two days later a tiny island appeared as a darker smudge on the horizon. Crusoe-like, we shaded our eyes against the fierce glare of the tropical sun. Impatiently we endured the interminable interval as our feebly flapping canvas made the best use it could of the fast-failing airs – all there was to propel us tediously towards fresh water – and our destiny. Creeping cautiously through the opening in the coral reef, we saw several small sharks. Turtles as well. Lunch wasn't far away. From under the shade of the palm trees fringing the beach, a freshwater stream trickled enchantingly over the rocks onto the dazzling white sand. We were marooned on a desert island.

"What a wonderfully exciting adventure," I said joyously to my companions. "I wonder if they do this for everybody, or have we just been lucky to be shipwrecked?"

I've never been good at putting jokes over.

Joseph.

No one seemed pleased that only the skilled seamanship of three seasoned Seychellois sailors had saved us from the same fate as those hapless hens.

The tiny island proved bigger than first we thought. Tropical, yes. Deserted, no. It had radio communication and an airstrip. No supermarket at which to replenish our food stocks.

Roasted, fried, spiced, stewed, soup; the cook did his best as we sampled every possible way of serving turtle.

Forty-eight hours later, an engineer flew in from Belgium. After less than a minute poring over the engine, he rather shamefacedly informed the skipper that the part he'd brought with him was wrong. We waited overnight for the right one.

Joyce.

By the time all was fixed, Joseph was swearing he'd never sail again. I was fed up too. Saltwater showers don't noticeably relieve perpetual perspiration, but at least we had fresh drinking water. The other couple sat under the deck awning eating hot red peppers, aloof, pretending they were enjoying it all.

We did visit several islands and atolls where the wildlife was wonderfully diverse. The giant tortoises of Aldabra were remarkable. Measuring a metre in length, with a huge domed shell, and weighing about three hundred and fifty kilos, they ignored humans as they ponderously promenaded on their short, fat, scaly legs.

The many species of land and sea birds were endlessly watchable. Sundry terns, tropic birds, frigate birds and blue-footed boobies cruised over the sea and shoreline. Inland, sunbirds and other brightly coloured avian wonders whistled, screeched and trilled in the dense tropical foliage. Our tick-list would drive your average birdwatcher to distraction. Snorkelling around the picture-postcard islands and coral reefs was utterly magical, as we swam nonchalantly among the spectacular shoals of multicoloured tropical fish.

The delays caused by the breakdown curtailed our voyage as we had to be back on Mahé to catch our scheduled flight home. We never did reach Comoros. Joseph, who said he was bloody glad to get his feet back on dry land, wanted to sue them.

I couldn't have enjoyed it more. It was exciting and fun.

Joseph.

That farcical excursion set me back £5,300!!!

Of course I wanted to sue. We visited the tour office in Aberdeen but it was clearly a hole-in-the-wall operation and satisfaction would be minimal. We got a cheque for two hundred pounds.

I've never set foot on a small sailing vessel since. Nor shall I!

*

ICELAND'S VOLCANOES AND GLACIERS

Joyce and I had long cherished a wish to visit Iceland. In the merry month of May 1996, we were enjoying the pleasant spring climate of Mallorca.

Sitting at breakfast in our campervan one morning, Joyce was dowsing as usual with her pendulum. By now, this was her regular method of contacting her spirit guides.

"Hmmm," she muttered absently. "We have to go to Iceland."

I choked on my toast and spilt hot coffee on my shorts and bare knees.

"Oww! Ahh! What!***? When!***?" I have never encouraged the use of impolite expletives in our household, however…

"Now," she said, slipping the silvery sliver of quartz back into its chamois leather pouch and getting to her feet. "Soon as we can."

"But we've only been here about three weeks. We said at least a month. There's still stuff to do here."

"NOW," she spoke sharply this time. "You know very well when the guides say NOW they don't mean tomorrow; or next week. Drink your coffee and start packing up the gear. I know you spilt it, clumsy. There's a drop more in the pot."

It was only later I realised I would soon be standing on the flank of an active volcano that lay on, or very close to, the compass bearing we had been given when working on that globe-encircling ley line in Kenya* the previous year.

Iceland? June? Ideal weather. Why not?

With the van packed and (me) wearing clean shorts, I headed for the ferry and we were soon landing at Denia, on the Spanish mainland. No autoroute for us, just the old coast road winding through villages and towns, until we turned north for Andorra and the Pyrenees. It was a leisurely trundle along all the back roads we could find – our preferred way of crossing any great distances.

Once home, we quickly changed from Mediterranean mode to suitably sub-Arctic and headed for Aberdeen and the ferry that would take us north to the Faroe Isles and the vessel that ran between Denmark and Iceland.

Friends who lived near us in Wales had visited Iceland a couple of times, pursuing their botanical and ornithological interests, but they used their Land Rover camper conversion; a rugged 4 x 4 if ever there was one. They had reported that the only road around Iceland was just a sort of causeway of volcanic ash and the only vehicles one would meet were super-high-ground-clearance Japanese four-wheel-drives. The only problem then, was that our camper van, built on a Fiat chassis, had front wheel drive and low ground clearance. I had always insisted it was not a feasible idea to take it to Iceland.

Joyce, as usual, came up with the solution. "Do as you're told and trust your angels," she said. Well, I do trust them but, even so, there were to be one or two hairy moments in the next few weeks.

After disembarking from the ferry at Seydisfjordur, a port at the eastern extremity of the island, we hit the road – or perhaps the road hit us! What roads! Much as our friends had warned us. A ribbon of black ash with a rough and tumble of moss- and lichen-covered volcanic rocks on either side. When we stopped to admire a view, we were quite overcome by the stillness and the silence.

The junction at which we stopped for our first night was where a branch road led to the first of the magnificent waterfalls we planned to visit. On our arrival, there had been a 'Road Closed' sign and we had felt this to be a major setback. However, even as we sat at breakfast next morning, along came some men in a truck and behold, the sign was gone! We moved on a mile or so and we could hear it long before we saw it.

Dettifoss, described as Europe's mightiest waterfall. In the midst of a barren landscape slashed across by a huge basalt-cliffed canyon littered with glacial rubble, appeared this most spectacular and powerful sight. Being in such total isolation and lacking the commercialism of Iguaçu or Niagara, this was all the more awe-inspiring.

The road then took us through green grass and a few newly leafing birch trees, along coastal cliffs with beautiful seascapes, and the screaming of gulls as we passed near a nesting colony. Further on, Joyce asked me to stop the 'van as we were spellbound by the sight of so many shades of green on the mountains. Some brilliant, others darker, still others more delicate; they enriched the landscape with their generous splashes of colour.

On through lava fields, boiling mud pools and sulphur springs. Now the colours had changed due to the mineral deposits left around the perimeters of the pools. From greyish white, through golden sandy shades to aquamarine and other varying hues of blues and pinks and greens.

The overall mood or atmosphere that we felt along the northern part of the island was one of peace and tranquillity. However, as we left Reykjavik, the capital, at the western end, we knew we could expect something rather different. Occupying almost the extreme westernmost part of the island is a glacier-covered mountain, the Snaefellsjökull and, surrounding its foot, lie the fields of lava that would have been overflowing from its peak in its active period, many thousands of years ago.

Quite close to the capital stands Hekla, a very recent addition to Iceland's long list of volcanoes. As we set about climbing the steep slope for a view of its snow-capped peak, the first bird we saw was a merlin. It was a pleasure to know that the species was prospering here.

Hekla is the mountain I mentioned as lying very close to the ley line from Kenya, crossing Spain on its Great Circle pathway. We spent a few hours there in deep meditation, as indicated by the oscillations of Joyce's shining silver sliver.

Now for our only navigational error of the whole trip.

Not that there were many opportunities for going wrong, especially as, with our front wheel drive, we dared not venture off the 'road' onto dirt or rock tracks. Well, this time on reaching a fork which, I have to say in my defence, was not too clearly sign-posted; in fact, there was no sign-post; instead of asking Joyce to use her pendulum again, I opted to go left, leaving, we discovered later, a power station and a small community hidden in a fold in the mountain to our right. After following the road for many miles across a vast tundra plateau, we decided we must have got it wrong and returned to the aforementioned fork. On taking the alternative, we crossed over the sizeable river and discovered the hidden power station and village. Again, there was no choice; just one road passing through and out the other side. Following this, we soon realised it was not what one could expect of the main road, but for at least half an hour there was simply nowhere wide enough to turn around. Then, blocking the track before us, was a row of four huge steel drums. A hundred metres beyond the drums was a really massive sloping ramp of rock, clearly impassable for us.

I, though I say it myself, skilfully executed a five- or six-point turn and we retraced our route to the junction and resumed our journey.

A few kilometres farther and we were at the double-drop waterfall at Gullfoss. In this land of outstanding spectacle, Gullfoss was, for me, pre-eminent and we were only two of the many visitors that day, watching awe-struck, as unimaginable thousands of gallons of water thundered over the massive rock fault, the veils of spray refracting the sunshine into brilliant rainbows.

All to soon we had to think of heading east, along the southern coast road, passing under the gargantuan mass of the Vatnajökull. This is the most voluminous ice cap in Iceland, and one of the largest in area in Europe. It is the largest protected area in Europe and is believed by many to be the most beautiful place on earth.

This, Joyce declared, was the principle reason for our presence on Iceland. though the full significance we did not learn until after returning home.

*

Later we once more sat for a meditation, this time directed to Oraefelljökull, the highest point of the enormous Vatnajökull glacier. These names and places we recorded in some detail at the time but their significance was not borne home to us until several weeks later.

Joyce assured me afterwards that, at some thirty-five minutes, this was one of my longest sessions in trance as well as being, to her eyes, the most profound and concentrated.

We stayed overnight at the side of the snowmelt outflow, listening to the grinding and groaning of the huge blocks of ice as they jostled each other for position on their slow race to the nearby Norwegian Sea.

Another reason for our trip was to widen our knowledge of the birds here. The climate of the region regulates the range of residents on this island but our visit had proved quite fruitful, with over thirty species added to our list.

Next day we boarded our homeward-bound ferry, the Smyrill, at Seydisfjordur and we too headed south into the icy Norwegian Sea.

POSTSCRIPT

Shortly after settling in back at home we learned from radio and television newscasts that volcanologists were getting seismic information leading them to predict a volcanic eruption of the Oraefelljökull, the highest point of the Vatnajökull glacier in southern Iceland, to which I referred earlier. It was one of the locations to which we had specifically directed energy in our meditations. It seemed that the magma beneath the mountain covered by this, the largest glacial cap in Europe, was rising up ready for an eruption. It was melting the underside of the glacier with the potential for vast quantities of melt water to run back into the volcano. If/when ice-cold water reached magma, the pressure under which the trapped, super-heated steam would be held, could result in a colossal eruption. The staggering power generated would probably blow the top of the mountain clean off.

As you might by now expect, we sat in meditation, directed our concentration towards this matter and asked our questions. In the response, we were asked to meditate daily for one week, channelling in Cosmic energy in collaboration with our friends in the Angelic Realm and the Elemental Kingdoms, with a view to mitigating the seriousness of the devastation – and keep watching this space.

Sure enough, as the week went by, the subject fell further and further back in news-headline priority. The scientists could offer no explanation how or why the flow of the melt-water under the icecap had either reduced or altered its flow in some way.

Three days after the week was up, there was an eruption. It was not as severe as had been expected. People and animals had been moved from the path of any volcanic outpourings and damage was limited to the comparatively few buildings in that path. As the silt and mud flowed to the sea, the road and some bridges were either swept away or buried. No lives were lost.

So, why did we go to Iceland? What were we doing there if it were not to prevent or at least reduce the scale of such an event?

Then we learned that on 30th September the seismometers detected the beginning of an eruption under the Vatnajökull icecap. On the fifth of November 1996, the meltwater burst vertically from two kilometres above the tongue of the glacier. The summit of the mountain, along with its glacial cap, remained intact.

The resulting flood obliterated a 376-metre-long bridge, the majority of a second bridge, nine hundred metres in length, twelve kilometres of roadway and twenty-three power-line towers, causing fourteen million US dollars in damage, while adding seven square kilometres to the area of Iceland. <u>But, there were no fatalities or injuries, and the flood did not reach any nearby settlements.</u>

This information is readily available on the internet, which tells us that, in previous centuries, eruptions had caused considerable damage and taken their toll on human life. A major eruption in 1362 was, historically, Iceland's largest explosive eruption. Another eruption occurred during 1727-28. Both eruptions were accompanied by <u>major glacier outburst floods that caused both serious property damage and numerous fatalities.</u>

Though we did not know this, we were not alone in bringing energy to this geological event. About the same time, other people around the world were receiving psychic information concerning what was undoubtedly the same situation. It was some months before there came into my possession, a copy of the well-established English weekly periodical, *Psychic News*, No. 3358, dated Saturday, October 19, 1996. This carried a front-page double headline *"ICELAND VOLCANIC ERUPTION FULFILS PSYCHIC PROPHECY."*

*For much more information on this and other remarkable stories of our world travels, see Amazon/Kindle *A MARRIAGE*, available to download or purchase in paperback.

ME – AND JAMAR

My immediate sensation is profound shock. I am suddenly and unexpectedly confronted by a person from the past. The shock is all the more powerful as this is an individual whom I last saw, around sixteen years ago, in an emotionally violent confrontation.

I am white Caucasian, Anglo-Irish, now in my ninetieth year, of slight physique.

He is black Afro-American, some ten years my junior. He is still athletically broad and strong.

When last we met, we'd been acquainted for some three or four years; that is to say, from some months before the millennium, which we celebrated together among mutual friends. Gathered, for the occasion, on the patio of a villa in the coastal mountains of southern Spain, near Gibraltar, we sip our late evening drinks, and watch the lights of Morocco shimmering across the Straits. The Straits of Gibraltar guarded by the Pillars of Hercules away to our right.

Apart from the chirruping of cicadas, the only sound disturbing the silence, the sort of comfortable silence that can exist between friends, is the muted thumping of diesels, as a couple of small oil-tankers crawl across the seascape. Idly I wonder from which Arab state they have come; which northern European ports are destined to receive their cargoes of black gold. Perhaps my son, an officer in the Merchant Navy, is aboard one of them.

The civilised world, to which we belong, is in a turmoil of disputes. Disputes motivated by man's thirst for – whatever it is that possesses and motivates… Well, for the moment, our small group is not concerned with the mundane.

Each one of our group of a dozen or so, a mixture of ages, of the sexes, of widely diverse ethnic origins, has committed to a life of service to the world and our fellow humans. In a word, we call ourselves Spiritualists. We recognise and acknowledge the racial and religious conflicts that beset our world and we have, quite independently, dedicated our lives to that service. It is this commitment, mutually recognised, that has brought us together.

However, there is, unrecognised by the others, an undercurrent of unease between two of us. I, the white Caucasian, and Jamar, the black Afro-American, though outwardly manifesting the conviviality of the occasion, have good reason for our own conflict. Not only are we, in physical, earthly terms, from contrasting ethnic origins; in spiritual terms, scarcely understood and accepted by most humans at this stage of the evolutionary cycle of our solar system, we are from opposing factions in the antediluvian struggle for control of the Milky Way Galaxy.

Through a somewhat unusual series of events in my life, I have followed the clichéd path of near-rags to near-riches. My own coastal villa, located some hundred and fifty kilometres to the west, is occupied by the Afro-American. He is a qualified and practising doctor of

Macrobiotic medicine. Living with him is his Norwegian partner who is not the mother of his four children, two of whom, in their early 'teens, also live with him in my villa. The other two, already in their twenties, have apartments close to where their Indian mother lives, in nearby Fuengirola.

Jamar, for reasons not clear to me at the time, has had the misfortune to find himself in straitened circumstances that have left him and his two younger children in imminent likelihood of being evicted; put out on the street. My villa – we use it as a residential centre for Spiritual healing – is the obvious solution and I arrange that the family move in there, so that the two functions can operate to mutual benefit.

Only later do I realise the significance of a major factor in this scenario. My wife, Joyce, and I work as healers in our Centre and other healers practice here too. All of us offer our services free of any charge. Jamar, on the other hand, charges for his professional services as well as for the food he supplies as part of his Macrobiotic treatments.

I also learn, from mutual acquaintances, that some of Jamar's earlier activities along the coast have not always been strictly honest and ethical. And so, the first seeds of doubt and distrust are sown.

Over two years later, I learn from a Spanish acquaintance, who has extensive knowledge and experience in the field of Spanish property law, that if I allow Jamar to continue in his occupancy of my villa for the next few months, without any legally established rental agreement and payment, he can acquire a right of possession equivalent, I suppose, to what we in Britain would term 'squatters' rights.'

There is quite a lot of my money tied up in that villa. Money which my own children might reasonably expect to inherit. Can I afford to see this misappropriated by someone whose scruples, one might say, leave something to be desired? No, I cannot allow this to happen. I have family commitments which I cannot ignore. Even as a committed and conscientious Spiritualist, my brotherly love does not stretch to that.

When approached for an explanation, Jamar makes it clear to me that he is arrogantly confident of his position. He has no intention of vacating the villa. I have no alternative but to invoke Spanish law and involve local police in the unpleasant task of physically ejecting this family and their possessions from my property. Yes, unpleasant indeed, although no physical violence transpires.

On that day, on a phone line – he was in Norway at the time – with this supposedly spiritual person, a man versed and practised in the esoteric and arcane; a man with whom I have accompanied departing souls on their walk of death; a man whose liquor-fuelled violence and domineering personality have become more obvious in recent months; screaming down the phone, he verbalises his barely suppressed anger and frustration:

"For what you are doing to me and to my children, I will see that you pay; I will follow you to your grave and beyond, though it take ten thousand years."

Sixteen years have passed since that dramatic occasion on the Costa del Sol.

Today, I am sitting deeply relaxed, yet expectant, in this quiet room overlooking Cardigan Bay. As my mind eases into quiet contemplative meditation…

Without warning, he enters to sit and face me. I see, once more, the anger, the violence, the domineering and manipulative man I had thought to befriend. I recall, instantly, my last evaluation of this person; alcohol-dependant, paranoid schizophrenic, given on occasion to physical violence towards his partner. His demeanour suggests I might expect the same.

I deliberately seek strong, confident eye contact. Not difficult. He is already directing these same characteristics my way. Neither of us is going to back down. I shiver. My back-hairs rise. I realise the shiver is beyond anything I have ever known.

I recognise that Jamar, with whom I worked for several years at a deeply spiritual level, is projecting his frustrated anger and his potential for powerful violence, in a way I have never before experienced. I confront this imminent threat with a resolve of my own.

Forgiveness is the first sentiment that I return towards the implacability I now face. Sorrow for the situation that now exists between us. Regret that we seem unable to resolve this. I try to convey to him the impropriety of his earlier actions; things could have gone forward so differently.

Suddenly, I realise that there is a profound connection between the emotional pain this situation brings, and the physical pain swirling into my consciousness. The agony of earlier years of spinal disorder, almost forgotten; for who can remember the sensation of pain after it has gone? The suffering from my damaged stomach. Bumps and cuts and burns, seemingly trivial perhaps, but all part of the pattern of learning that derives from pain, whether physical or emotional. For is it not through pain and suffering that most of life's lessons are learned? Physical pain is but the manifestation of the emotional and spiritual pain that we endure as we pass through this so-called vale of tears.

Now, with these thoughts flooding my mind, I search for their reflection in the eyes that are challenging me from a few feet away. Momentarily, my hopes rise, as those eyes seem to reflect my own pain and regret. I urgently regenerate my earlier thoughts of unconditional love and forgiveness, projecting them with all the power of my mind. I desperately want to bring to an end this emotional and spiritual barrier that has come between us. In the earlier years, we had worked so well together, bringing physical, emotional and spiritual healing to lost and struggling souls.

In return, I am receiving an impression that there can be no love; there can be no forgiveness. Our conflict, as we both know, is not between personalities, has nothing to do with racial ethnicity. These are mere human symptoms manifesting in this lifetime. It has its origins somewhere deep in creation's history and, yes, it can go on for ten thousand years; ten times ten thousand; whatever it takes – even unto the end of...

My conscious mind is struggling to intervene. I open my eyes; I wonder to myself; this is bizarre. The only possible reason why Jamar has forced his way past my protection, is that he has come to let me know he has passed over.

Today, he is leaving me in no doubt.

He will be waiting for me…on the other side. Waiting to renew our conflict.

And who will be the ferryman?

I shiver again…

*

JAMAR – AND ME

I've got him!

He forgot to protect himself before opening his energy field to meditate.

He's in an open-energy environment. Damme, he's always avoided that.

This time I've really got him!

Ever since 2003, our skirmish, I been waiting for this chance. Those guys he's with now; there's only one of 'em would know what I'm talking about.

Yeah, the fat one with the white whiskers.

But he's no problem; he works at least one vibratory octave away from Joseph.

I'd better not waste time here.

Joseph's pretty damn smart and he'll soon be on to me.

Sloppy. Not like him to miss the protection routine.

I wanna let him know I'm still around and gunning for him, even though I passed over 'bout a year back.

In fact, the stupid dude is making it easy for me.

I can take him out right now.

We can have the showdown right here, on this side. This is going to be r-e-a-l sweet.

Goddammit! He's on to me.

Hell, I was enjoying this, and now it's too damn late.

I shoulda gone to Spacesavers. They coulda set up a distortion lens between us, then he wouldn't have felt me.

Boy, did he get that protection pillar up in a hurry. I always had him down as a wised up kinda guy, but that was r-e-a-l f-a-s-t.

Now I'll have to wait until he does cross over.

GOD alone knows when that'll be. HE keeps finding jobs for the guy so he doesn't have to come over here.

Still, his body can't last much longer, can it?

CAN IT?

He' gotta be way over eighty by now.

Must've been mid-nineties we met.

I'd done a Spiritualism spot on one of the Spanish TV channels.

Managed to get quite a bit in on the Macrobiotics stuff too, 'cos that was my specialty. Nice little earner.

Anyway, this Joseph guy and his wife, they got my number from the TV folk and they called me up. Said they had a Spiritual Healing Centre up in the hills, back of town.

Town was Fuengirola, Costa del Sol, España.

I'd been operating around there about twenty-five years but, somehow, the pesetas didn't seem to come my way as much as I would've liked.

Fact is, I was pretty well broke a lot of the time. Life wasn't too good back around then.

My Indian wife had left me. The two older girls sorta lived between her apartment and their own. The younger two, boy and a girl in their 'teens were living with me and this thirty-something Norwegian piece who took a fancy to me on one of my trips up there, coupla years back.

For all I was coming up to sixty, I kept pretty damn fit.

I was big in the local athletics scene and ran classes and events all over Spain.

That didn't pay much either.

Time came, the guy who owned the apartment in town started getting a bit assy over a few weeks' rent.

Another thing, didn't help much – I had a real taste for Bushmills.

Yeah, stoned most all of the time – and broke the rest.

Then, just before the Millennium, out of the beautiful, blue, Spanish sky, there's this coupla Limeys.

Perfect pushovers!

Healers, they said. Got this centre up there in the hills. Couldn't have me and the kids out on the street, could they? Against their Spiritual principles.

Perfect!

So, we moved in, lock, stock and barrel. Easy as kiss my fanny.

Nice place it was. Plenty of room, nice gardens, usual pool, the works.

Worth a few greenbacks, I reckoned.

Yeah, we did quite a bit of work, separate and together. I taught Joseph some of my stuff; even some of the West African tribal stuff I got from my slavery folks, back in the US of A.

Hell, he even bought me an itty-bitty car.

But we didn't really get on.

And we both knew why.

Then I found out something real special.

We were all at a party to see in the New Millennium. It was at a friend's villa down the coast towards The Rock.

Quite spectacular in a way, with the lights of some Moroccan town across the Straits and a couple of small oil tankers chugging past; probably on their way to some port up in the north.

Only about ten or twelve of us – healers and Spiritualists I already knew, including Joseph and his healer-wife Joyce. Hadn't taken her long to figure me out, dammit. We'd had some food, I remember, and were on the patio having a few drinks when I found myself talking to a guy I'd never met before.

Turned out he'd been invited by one of the girls who worked out of Joseph's place. She did tarot and crystals or something.

He was a detective-inspector from the local Guardia Civil, which is their sort of high-level, semi-military, police force *en España*.

Well, we talked awhile and he mentioned that this girlfriend had told him about how I'd come to be living in the villa.

It was him wised me up on a few things. Why he didn't like Joseph, I don't know. Maybe it was just a social class thing.

Said if I carried on living in Joseph's place, without any paperwork or rent and stuff, for three years, I could claim a legal right of ownership. Sort of legal theft.

Huh?

How about that?

I guess it took a while to sink in.

I'd pulled one or two stunts up and down the coast and made a few bucks here and there.

But this – man, this could set me up in some style.

Things carried on as before for a while.

Joseph and his wife went back home to the UK, like they did most years. I never really knew what they got up to. I was too busy keeping my own family ship afloat. They sometimes traveled worldwide in that fancy camper of theirs. Stinking rich.

Then sometimes, I would go off to Norway with my partner and run Macrobiotics clinics for groups up there. It helped pay the bills.

It was a few weeks before one of these trips was coming up, when Joseph came to me and said he wanted to draw up some paperwork to do with the villa and I would have to start paying some rent.

Hah! No way, José.

Thanks to my acquaintance at the Millennium party, I'd been expecting something like this. I knew Joseph was an educated guy and guessed he'd figured this one out with the help of his own Spanish friends.

First time, I sorta shrugged it off; said I was happy the way things were.

Second time, he was showing some attitude. I could tell he must have friends, probably lawyers or somesuch, had put him wise.

Turned out later, a former lady business partner of mine'd put Joseph and his wife on to Elias, who worked in the property department at the local town hall.

When I left for Norway, things were pretty much stalemate and that three-year term had only months to run. I put it out of my mind.

Next thing, I'm up there in Oslo and I get a crazy phone call from my son. I'd left him at the villa with a pal, so they could look after things.

Seven in the morning; the boys were still in their beds, when Joseph and Elias, along with Luis, a strong-arm from Peru, came into the house, rousted the boys out of bed and told them to get the hell out.

The locks had already been changed.

I yelled at my son to call B, my detective-inspector friend, and get him to come over and sort it out.

Dammit, Elias was one step ahead.

He'd already called the Policia Local; their office was just a few kilometres away.

The two uniforms who turned up were Elias's pals in the Town Hall. B was there.

Seems they told B it wasn't a criminal matter; he had no jurisdiction, and he better leave the premises. ***Pronto, por favor.***

O' course, I only got the story later, from the boys. Never saw B again.

The Policia gave them thirty minutes to collect their belongings and get out.

How the hell were they supposed to do that? The place was full of all the family's stuff. Clothes and computers and… kitchen stuff…and…dammit…everything.

As they were leaving, my son called me again and filled me in with the details. I yelled for him to give the phone to Joseph and we exchanged what he would call "a few heated words and phrases."

Stuck-up bastard.

Bullshit! I cursed him to Hell and back. He didn't need the goddamn villa.

Not like I needed it.

I ended up telling him, for what he was doing to me and my kids, I would surely make him pay.

Even to the grave and beyond; even beyond beyond.

He knows I can, too.

He knows I'm Extra-terrestrial. Dragon and Reptilian, from the Draco and Orion Constellations.

But, I'm not one of the nice guys. I'm not from the fifth-dimension-evolved-races that, right now, are Earthborn to remedy negative influences from past reptilian beings, and expose the matrix stuff.

Until I transitioned, I was just one of many thousands of shape-shifted reptilians who remain on Earth to resist that movement.

He knows as well as I do we both chose this time around to set up a showdown. All this villa stuff was just the preliminaries – a trial of strength sort of.

Yeah, a battle he won; but he better watch out – the war ain't over yet.

I didn't want to leave; to pass through the veil; but I had no choice.

The human, physical body is thousands of years away from being perfect.

Guess I didn't always look after mine when I had it.

Could be, they'll never get it right. Then there'll have to be another showdown. Global destruction and re-start.
All over again. Like Atlantis style.
Guess that's when we'll move in and take over.
Just like we've been aiming to for aeons.

Now this Joseph guy?
Ain't he just something else.
He's Pleiadean. One of those with the job of seeding new worlds with the essence of evolved human form, and working with a planet's consciousness and its existing life so as to introduce new beings and ideas.
Guess it's no wonder he always acted like his head was right up his own arse.
Yeah, it'll be just like Atlantis and Lemuria all over again.

Guess we're both into this stuff.
But I got him figured.
It won't be over between us until one of us settles it.
Once and for all time.
That was a pretty lousy stunt he pulled with me and my kids. My wife was pretty damn upset when they turned up on her doorstep.
This has got real personal.
He knows I'll be waiting for him.
I can be very patient.
It's a lesson I learned in my time on Earth – and I was there a long time.

You could say Joseph is the author of his own destiny…

… and *I* will be the ferryman …

… and **HE WILL PAY** the ferryman …

… and the oboloscoin[1] is obsolete …

Ha-Ha-ha-ha-ha-ha-ha-ha-ha-

ha-ha-ha-ha-haaa . . . .

*

---

[1]oboloscoin – coin placed under the tongue of the recently dead as payment for being ferried across the River Styx to reach Hades. Charon is the ferryman. Without the correct fee, he will not take the dead across, and they will be forced to wander the banks of the Styx… **_for eternity_**…aha-ha-ha-ha-haaa

AFTERLIFE

One week, in my writing class, we were set a homework on afterlife –'no definite article.' I was with them again when people discussed their first drafts. One erred on the side of frivolity – imaginary happenings out of his body but still earthbound. The other, an unexpected interpretation of 'life after life;' the second 'life' being a fifteen years 'life' prison sentence. I decided I'd be more focused, more comprehensive. Not to disparage their interesting work.

'Afterlife' is a lower-case composite noun like 'afterbirth' – a physical object. Separate the two nouns and everything changes. 'After birth' raises an abstract concept of 'what happens after the process of birth ?" Applying this principle to 'afterlife' the question becomes 'what happens after a life…has ended?'

First a brief thought on 'before life.' We have no choice at the physical, or biological, level since our mammalian conception is the outcome of parental activity over which we have no control. After the difficult process of passing through the birth canal: 'birth' – we have no recollection of any 'before'.

We arrive in this world unprepared,
Pink skinned, rosy cheeked, golden
haired.

Without any clue
As to what we would do
If from measles and mumps we were
spared.

It's later we ask whence we came
To seek out our fortune and fame.
But it's trouble and strife
To the end of our life.
And just what is the end game?

So now, near the end of the line,
I still worry 'bout life, about time.
I do try so hard
But I'm only a bard
So just pass me one more gin and
lime. @ Joseph Westlake

Not just amusing verses. Read between the lines.

Someone said to me, "What if we don't go – don't want to go." At the physical level, there is no 'if we don't go...' But we might ask 'to where does our soul or spirit go...?' There is what some scientists call *irrefutable evidence* of other dimensions, although their ranks are liberally sprinkle with atheists, too. No matter what spiritual procedures or religious practices we may have followed, after the inevitability of physical 'death' there ensues the inescapable experience of continuing existence, in my view. What follows is my imaginative opinion.

What are my qualifications for asserting this opinion?

I am a fairly old man and I've dedicated the second half of this lifetime, as well as many earlier lifetimes, to working with Spirit around the world. I have 'clinically died' twice and had a few other close calls with death. Thirty-five years ago, doctors predicted early confinement to a wheel chair and possibly a limited life-span. I, in consultation with my guides, decided otherwise. I am now nearer ninety than eighty years of age; I walk upright and comparatively unaided, although I do have physical health problems which are treated with medicines; I am currently involved in a spiritual movement aimed at improving life on earth. My mind seems unaffected by the passing of the years – but then, I would say that, wouldn't I? These theories have stood the test of my experiences.

Our 'next' level is widely known, esoterically, as the *astral plane.* And we have no choice! Before we left last time to incarnate, we were issued with a *return ticket.*

A biblical reference – "In my Father's house, there are many mansions." Hardly a suggestion of grand dwellings of bricks and mortar. Rather, as in the case of so many statements attributed to Jesus, an allegorical allusion open to interpretation; in this reading to various levels of vibratory existence as mentioned above.

Personally, I've encountered so many experiences that I believe with absolute certainty that: –

a) there is continuity of a form of life for every individual after the soul/spirit/life-force leaves the third dimensional incarnation; the physical body.

b) In this state of afterlife, the lower self, having vacated the incarnate physical vessel, the human body, re-joins the higher self. Now in a Limbo, decisions are made in communion with others, as to the future progression of the individuated spirit.

c) What follows is termed re-incarnation. Only after innumerable repetitions of this experience over an incalculable, uncomprehendible time period does the individuated spirit become re-absorbed into the vibratory level we term God, Creator, Divine Spirit, Source; of which it has, throughout this whole series of experiences, eternally been a part.

In other words, it might be said that each one of us is an indestructible extension of the eternal divine experience. You and I and everybody else, are GOD.

There were times in the not too distant past when one could be burned at the stake for making such a statement. Within my lifetime, at least one well-known public figure has been ostracised for using similar words (David Icke).

I've found no vast pool of knowledge of life after life, no one having returned to report on it. The internet carries detailed information on this concept as offered by a number of religious organisations. For myself, the perception most acceptable to me as probable is that arising in the eastern tradition and known as *kamaloka*. After all, it seems probable that no matter what religion we may profess on earth, in afterlife we all go through the same experience. This is illustrated by the following anecdote:

A few centuries ago there was a holy war in the Middle East.

A Christian and a Muslim who'd disliked each other on sight, fought ferociously on the principle that each said only <u>his</u> religion could save the world; only people of <u>his</u> religion would be eligible to go to heaven, to paradise.

They fought all that day and into the night, until both were utterly exhausted; and both died of their terrible wounds. They met at the Pearly Gates and each started grumbling and shouting at St Peter about the presence of the other. This went on for some time and it was getting quite noisy. St Peter began to lose patience. Exasperated, he spoke:

"Will you two…" He had to shout to make himself heard.

"Will you two shut up. Just look at the queue; it's half way round the world. You're holding everybody up!"

God heard all the rumpus and came to the gates.

"Hey, Pete." Remember they've known each other a while.

"Hey Pete. What's all the fuss about?"

The Christian shoved St Peter out of the way.

"God..." He was still shouting and raving. *"God, how could you let sinners like Muslims into heaven? This person didn't accept Jesus as his saviour in his lifetime."*

The Muslim, not to be outdone, shouldered the Christian out of his way.

"God..." He was shouting even louder. *"God, Christians don't deserve heaven. They are too proud and they disrespect your prophet Muhammad whom you sent to show us the way."*

God gestured for calm and quiet while he took his time over this one. After much consideration, he said,

"Neither of you has understood a thing in your lifetimes. Now, Muslim, I am sending you back on earth, and this time you will be a Christian.

And Christian, you will go back as a Muslim.

Now, both of you, TRY AND GET IT RIGHT THIS TIME, FOR CHRISSAKE!!!"

He turned to St Peter – *"Ah to be sure, to be sure, guess we'll see 'em both again, pretty soon."*

He talks like that, you know, because He's Irish. C'mon. Everybody knows God's Irish…and a Catholic…and male.

*

Ah, *kamaloka*. Again, the internet has much to offer on this intriguing subject. Basically, *kamaloka* is seen as what happens after physical death; it is the space of the astral plane where one's spirit goes at the time it vacates the physical vehicle; or, as we say, when one dies. One might say it is the first station up the line. Eastern tradition postulates that it takes forty days for the spirit energy to irrevocably evacuate from the physical tissue. This raises an interesting thought as to difficulties that might arise in the context of the eastern funeral pyre or the western cremation, both of which customarily occur within a few days of 'death'. And we all know it's dangerous to put spirits on a fire!

We may call it life after death, or even *afterlife,* but in my view, it's just one of the first steps after the death of the physical body in this third dimension. It's in *kamaloka* the soul starts the transformation process; a process, the duration of which is variable dependent on many factors arising during the immediate past life and other precedencies, with particular reference to what we humans, struggling in our imposed ignorance, call our Spirituality.

This description of the *kamaloka* concept is much abridged.

And it all takes time. If one experiences a measurable time-span in each earth life and time in each phase of *kamaloka,* how can anyone postulate the non-existence of time? If time is an illusion on earth and they don't have time on the other side, then all concepts of life are illusory; there is no life either here or hereafter; all is a figment of someone's overactive imagination! Here one might refer to philosophers such as Thomas Aquinas and Aristotle. For more recent thinking Ayn Rand has asked: why is it "I think therefore I am" (René Descartes) when our thought capabilities happen after we begin to exist in the womb? Shouldn't it be "I am therefore I'll think"?

In the thinking and understanding of modern spiritism, since our mental body is the part of us that continues existence during afterlife, then mental faculties, or thought capabilities, happen before, and concurrent with, our conception and existence in the womb; hypotheses and even decisions concerning the future actions and activities of the newly conceived incarnate occur conceptually on the higher level. As one cycle of experience it takes time – maybe seventy to a hundred years. Perhaps not a great deal of time, but time.

Thus, I see that time is not an idle, unsubstantiated thought but, even as a circle, it **is**.

You can't leave Buddhism out of this worldview, either.

There is a story about four Zen Monks who decided to meditate silently for twenty-five years.

By nightfall on the first day, the candle began to flicker and went out.

The first monk said, "Oh, no! The candle is out."
The second monk said, "Aren't we not supposed to talk?"
The third monk said, "Why must you two break the silence?"
The fourth monk laughed and said, "Ha! That leaves two of us who didn't speak."

Two? Not many people know this but there was a fifth monk there.
"Ah," you ask, "What did the fifth monk say?"

We don't know yet; it was only twenty-four years and three-hundred and sixty-four days ago. Ask me again tomorrow.

*

A couple of years ago, a spiritual medium, without any question or prompt from me, turned to me and said: "The task you are working on will be completed in this lifetime."

A lifetime dedicated to working with Spirit will ensure that that lifetime will be just as long as is necessary to carry out the task or tasks that you agreed upon with your guides before coming into incarnation. That is lifetime enough because, as sure as God made little apples, you'll be around again before you know it. Just remember these words of the French philosopher Pierre Teilhard de Chardin: –

You are not a Human Being seeking a Spiritual Experience

You are a Spiritual Being having a Human Experience

Another compelling aspect of 'after life' is, can we 'earthbound' really communicate with the dead? There is literature on the subject of prearranging *post mortem* rendezvous for inter-planal, or inter-dimensional, communication but, although some mediums have claimed success, there seems to be no substantiated evidence of the phenomenon. Within our group there has been discussion of the matter and I anticipate with much interest, nay gleeful delight, the successful outcome of any such prearrangement. Since the irrevocable passage of *anno domini* (is that the same as time?) suggests I am likely to be next among us to transition (the spiritualist term for death), I feel it's high time to make a firm decision as to places, dates and times for such fascinating, and stimulatingly thought-provoking, metaphysical exercises.

As I've already discussed above, some claim that time does not exist even in this life – it is but an illusion.

I've also heard many a practising psychic medium claim that 'they don't have time on the other side', which seems more likely.

So, I ask myself, that being the case, how does one arrange a trans-dimensional rendezvous for some time in the future; (in the past is even more exciting) if time is an illusion? Such exercises should entail some physical manipulation or manifestation and not merely conscious telepathic or trance-communicated verbal greeting between the two 'worlds'; either of which methods I could describe as suspect. Then again, is one allowed time-out from *kamaloka* for such frivolous activities?

I really would like to tell you more, but I can't remember a thing from the last time I was there. Or the time before. Or the time before.

On the other hand, *if* I ever did come back *and* remember, I could pretend I was God…and no one would ever know…except God.

And being a lapsed Catholic, I can't help wondering what the penance for 'impersonating' God would be, when I presented *the return half of my ticket*. Of course, having lapsed, I would have been excommunicated by the Church but I like to think that He would overrule that decision and welcome me back, when I had 'done my time'. But how could I 'do time' if there is no time 'on the other side?

Next question, please …

*

For further fascinating reading, type 144,000 into your search engine.

*

THE CROAKING CONVICT'S LAST LAUGH

At one hundred and two years, seven months, two weeks, four days, fourteen hours, forty-three minutes and … counting, Harold Yardley knows, in his lucid times, that he is the oldest prisoner suffering from Alzheimer's in a British jail. The oldest prisoner fullstop. You might think he'd've forgotten how long he'd been 'inside': this stretch; the other times; altogether. But he can tell you all those stretches, to the minute – (he has said, to those who've wished to know, that extending the calculation to one-hundredths of a second would be tediously tiring without yielding information of value) – in his lucid times.

The dementia didn't begin until his ninety-eighth year. The Chronic Obstructive Pulmonary Disease (COPD) diagnosis, delayed by the delinquency of the prison authorities, a couple of years later. When the croaking, wheezing cough became uncontrollable, wracking his deteriorating body with painful paroxysms, they finally called the doctor.

"No rush. Old geezer hasn't got long, anyway, what's the point?"

So, on pills and puffers, he'll cough his lungs out, literally, through a few more months, maybe a year at most. Like many old lags, no family to care.

A practical joker since boyhood, he's got one more up his sleeve. "Perpetrating a reputation perpetuator" is how his unusual mind thinks of it. Better not leave it too long though. His skeletal old body's more dead than alive; his short-term memory's extending recall times; lucidity gaps are confusing him more often.

Prison has one advantage, at least; all the time you need for reading. He'd read his way through enough bumf on ageing to pass a med school exam in geriatrics. Time to get his skates on; get his mates back to work.

Born on the fifth of November 1907, the unusual personality traits he'd exhibited in his formative years had gone unrecognised for what they were. Happily, despite his birthdate and ancestral lineage, he's never displayed any of   the more colourful behaviours of Guy, his gunpowder-plotting ancestor,   such   as   a proclivity   for pyrotechnics. Well, not much; one or two of his more youthful escapades had bordered on that description. It was decades before the scientific world took an interest in him and   acknowledged   his   status   as   a   genius. A genius with exceptional talents and few inhibitions.

He'd been in school through the Great War and by September 3rd 1939, when German troops marched into Poland,   he   was serving the second   year of his current sentence in one of the country's more secure prisons. It was neither the first nor would it be the last occasion   of   his   detainment   at   His, later to become Her, Majesty's pleasure.

Albert, his brother, younger by two years, seven days,   two   hours   and   seven   minutes, also had manifested unusual   mental   aberrations.   In particular a pronounced form of alpha-numeric dyslexia –

later to prove the instrument of their ultimate undoing. While still at school Albert showed an interest in motor cars and other mechanical and electrical devices, such as locks and alarms, a subject in which his skills improved with the evolving technical revolution. In their teens and twenties, his skills behind the wheel and beneath the bonnet of the embryonic sporting automobile proved invaluable. Thus, their many successful, profitable jewellery heists (though, sadly, not all, since the acknowledged acme of success in their profession included not being caught).

In the brothers' earlier years, not much was known about the workings of the brains of unusual people like them. Savants, they were labelled, and psychiatrists and neuroscientists were only beginning to understand the abnormal behaviour of their synapses and other electrical connections. Mutations caused chemical dysfunctions; inexplicable irregularities and anomalies within their brains, their minds, their behaviour.

Harold and Albert, born into a life of privation and abuse, had taken refuge in a life of crime – highly specialised crime, distinguished from the usual in two respects: an absence of violence and the remarkable, disproportionately high value of their individual hauls. While the pacifist nature of their crimes might have earned some leniency in sentencing, their refusal to return the loot increased their time inside exponentially. Envious members of London's criminal underworld were heard to express the 'justice' of this, though at the time, none was aware of the identities of these secretive members of their fraternity.

Twenty-five years the judge had clobbered him with for his most recent offence. The irony of meting out this life sentence to an eighty-year-old wasn't lost on Harold. Vindictive. Not because the robbery had involved any violence, but because of his stubborn, 'insolent', refusal to say one word concerning the whereabouts of the proceeds, which were never recovered. Apart, that is, from what was found in his possession at the time of his arrest (of which more later). His and Albert's already lengthy criminal careers, the prosecutors suspected, included many undetected crimes, as well as those they failed to pin on the Yardleys.

Unfortunately for Harold his behavioural problems had, during his latest, lengthy confinement, become aggravated by the onset of Alzheimer's. More and more frequent outbursts of violence (colourfully verbal rather than effectively physical due to his advancing muscular deterioration), towards prison personnel and fellow inmates (reluctantly tolerated rather than severely punished, for the same reason) compounded the duration of his latest sentence.

Throughout their lives, interested specialists researched the unusual talents displayed by Harold and Albert. Not that Albert operated at anything like Harold's level, as he himself was only too well aware. Harold was the elder and the leader, always. Harold sometimes thought it strange that the same genetic source had produced such wildly differing cerebral mutations in himself and Albert, while leaving their younger sister, Alison, apparently unaffected.

In order to achieve success and pleasure in their nefarious, nocturnally practiced profession (for profession it surely was, [albeit with genuine philanthropic motivation]) the collaboration of a third person had been essential. Someone who could remain quiet and anonymous in the background, unobtrusively manipulating and managing the movement and profitable disposal of the, sometimes quite exciting, proceeds.

Alison, a most attractive and intelligent product of the same genes, seemingly immune to her brothers' cerebral 'problems', has had the good sense to comply with her brothers' carefully proffered proposition that she "seduce" (she blushed enchantingly when admitting [to her brothers, though to no-one else] to having not encountered serious resistance) (I apologise for the apparently split infinitive which is compromised by the preceding verb and the accompanying, qualifying 'not'; I find it difficult satisfactorily to resolve this particular instance while retaining the rhythm and balance of the bracketed phrase) and marry a handsome young man of mid-Eastern extraction whose family, to this day, occupy themselves by trading in the rarefied atmosphere of Hatton Garden. (See my other story *DIAMONDS ARE FOREVER – PERHAPS* in this anthology). In due course, their brother-in-law has been happy (certain indication of the depraved depths   of his   vile immorality) to provide invaluable   information, the   provision of   which served to enhance the success and profitability of each venture.

Harold's brother-in-law's brother, Ismael, is (was) a high-level operator in the Diplomatic Corps; hence the CD plates on his expensive, not to mention sportive, example of a certain Italian motor manufacturer's craft. Ismael, whose anonymity I have promised (in the interests of diplomatic harmony as well as avoidance of accusations of criminally guilty conduct from the prosecution, to which he would have pled diplomatic immunity anyway) to protect, is blessed with a memory the high-poweredness of which exceeds even that of his highly coveted automobile.

This (his memory, not his automobile) facilitates communication between him and Harold; all of which is conducted, during approved prison visits, by the verbal exchange of multiple, multi-digit-coded messages.

In the course of his diplomatic duties, Ismael travels to   various   European   and   mid-Eastern countries, including   that   of his ancestors. Switzerland too has always been happy to allow the diplomat freedom of access, especially as his banking activities seem to necessitate frequent visits to the financial institutions for which that country is renowned and on which its economy is reputed to have been built.

(The practice of maintaining the integrity of the infinitive, while admirable with regard to its adherence to linguistic convention, sometimes can have the irritating consequence of destroying, irrevocably, the balance and rhythm sought by the writer relentless in his ambition constantly to create perfect prose. [After having, myself, committed uncountable hundreds of thousands of words {and that's only in the English language} to the page, as well as having read substantially in English {naturally, England being the land of my birth}, as well as other {European} tongues]) I still harbour doubts as to the existence of such perfection (though I am committed, irrevocably [to trying to find, that is, as well as] to write).

(And, dear Reader, I am aware how old-fashioned my practice of parenthetic bracketage appears, but I defy you not to be both impressed and edified by its elegant clarity).

These arrangements have served Harold and his ageing associates well over many decades (the longevity of successful operations on the scale of, and of the proportion, that I describe, indicates the trust and collaborative skill of its members) and now plans were well advanced for their most daring and potentially highest yielding project.

*

They would have got clean away but for Albert's disastrous directional error:

1. They dump the stolen getaway car half a mile from the wholesale jeweller's premises and ...

2. leave the loot with Albert's wife in her car. I have not broken the rules of composition by introducing this hitherto unmentioned lady as she has participated in earlier heists (see Jane Austen, *Northanger Abbey* for the highest possible authority) and . . .

3. will hand the swag over to the CD man for . . .

4. clandestine transportation (even an operator with the talents unquestionably displayed by the CD man aforesaid has yet to master the skill [if, indeed, there is such a skill in the field of metaphysics] of bulk teleportation, especially since the volumes involved were substantially in excess of those alleged to have been successfully manipulated by certain Indian Holy Men in the latter half of the twentieth century [some of which were later shown to be fraudulent]), to Switzerland and. . .

5. subsequently to private international destinations forever to remain unknown.

6. They drive away in yet another car (a Jaguar stolen for the purpose).

7. Then, it all goes tits up: Albert, sometimes referred to with loving tolerance by his older brother as 'not the sharpest knife in the block,' in his excitement drives off too enthusiastically. Burning rubber as he takes a tight curve in a suburban street, he attracts the attention of a passing off-duty police inspector who (having already heard the distant clanging of the Winkworth bells [colloquially

termed 'gongs'], with which the Wolseley 6/80 cars, favoured, at that time, by the Metropolitan Police, were fitted) gives chase in his modest family saloon.

8. They're leaving the cop well behind and entering territory unfamiliar to Albert when Harold calls a right turn. This, Harold knows, will bring them onto a faster road with the certainty of losing the vainly pursuing policeman. Instead . . .

9. Albert hangs a left and in seconds they're trapped in a small industrial estate.

(This is a not unknown phenomenon: [I refer to Albert's directional confusion, not the being trapped in an industrial estate] indeed my own sister, [herself subject to frequent directional confusion] did exactly the same thing when taking her driving test some forty years ago – and passed "because", said the Ministry of Transport examiner, "you executed the manoeuvre, albeit in the opposite direction to that I had requested, precisely, safely, and with all the correct preliminaries," [though procedural preliminaries may not have been predominant in Albert's mind at the time.])

In custody at the local nick, apoplectic Harold and apologetic Albert are in suitably subdued mood. Later that night, in his interview with the young investigating officer, Albert explains again how they'd been celebrating a big win on the dogs at nearby Harringay. Hubristically, not having anticipated apprehension, Harold had not agreed any explanation, to be offered in the event of such misfortune, with Albert.

"In a stolen SS Jaguar?" retorts the detective, knowing Albert had been driving when they were arrested. "On a Thursday night? When they race only on Saturdays?" By now his chuckle has surpassed the status of repressibility. "Come now sir, we'll have to do better than that, won't we? I'll be back."

Minutes pass; many minutes. The detective returns. Without a word, watching Albert's face, he places two keys on the table in front of Albert.

Stony-faced, Albert's not giving anything away. He doesn't so much as blink.

"Albert, a colleague has been checking these two keys, officially logged as being in your possession at the time of your apprehension last night. While we've been chatting here, my colleague has further ascertained that these two very keys provide access to the outer security gates of the jeweller's premises situated close to where you were first sighted in that stolen, speeding car. Now then, minutes earlier, some person or persons unknown had used these very keys to gain access to those very premises and illegally removed a substantial quantity of jewellery and other valuables, the value of which, although currently unknown to me, is said to be considerable ...... (In the 1940s and 50s I served in the police so I can vouch for the stilted, prolix form of English employed by these servants of the Crown in 'interviews' and handwritten reports. Regrettably, I have been unable, myself, to lose the habit completely) … Yes, Albert. Your statement that you know nothing about the keys has been duly noted, but you can see where this is leading, can't you, so I have no alternative but to detain you on suspicion of… Yes, your 'no comment' is also noted. Now, unless you have anything to add, I'm going to talk to your brother."

Albert hides his face in his hands, not in despair but to conceal a rueful smile; he doesn't say aloud, "It's a fair cop, guv," like they do in balloons in the comic strips he still reads laboriously, unobtrusively (secretly actually), when alone in his room.

In his interview with Harold the young detective is more forceful. He now knows a lot more about the Yardley brothers, and poor Albert's dull-witted reputation contrasts strikingly with the reported high IQ of his older brother.

"It's no good, is it Harold? The diamond discovered in your left pocket and the ruby discovered in your right pocket make it quite clear. You're the brains and Albert's just the driver. What the hell (I paraphrase) did you take those two stones for, anyway?

(In this, an era prior to the introduction of electro-mechanical recording devices in police interrogations, the use of expletives and epithets not normally in polite use [and omitted from the subsequent handwritten summaries] could be offensive to the more refined ear.)

(I feel the historic remoteness of the earlier parts of my narrative demands explanation for the benefit of those who, familiar with electronic computing and word-processing technology, might find it difficult to comprehend the handicaps experienced in the furtherance of mid-twentieth century law-enforcement.)

"Expenses." Harold's nonchalant shrug and his serene, confident smile serve only to elevate the detective's blood pressure.

"Alright, so we know you got the gate keys from somewhere, but we haven't worked out how the dickens (I make no apology for paraphrasing) you did all the other locks. They're all combinations and number codes. We know you're a sort of genius with numbers, but how in the name of all that's holy (I paraphrase), did you find them out? That place has the best security in the blooming country, never mind this fabulous (again I paraphrase) city."

This time Harold's smile is less amused; more enigmatic. He had long ago discovered the usefulness of his unusual abilities.

'Remote viewing' is an esoteric psychic phenomenon known, in Harold's time, only to a privileged few. The alleged practice of seeking impressions about a distant or unseen target using extrasensory perception. During the war (which coincided with an earlier incarceration) high-ranking officers of Military Intelligence from UK, USA, USSR and

Israel visited Harold, seeking to exploit this little-understood talent.

Yes, along with his phenomenal mental skills, Harold can 'view' remotely. That, along with his eidetic, photographic memory, is how he accesses combinations and other information for breaching security alarms and locks. (In the interests of upholding my own lifelong ambition to maintain the lowest possible crime rate in our country, I don't intend to detail procedures for the acquisition of skills appropriate to the practice of this potentially [in its non-military context] lucrative hobby.)

From long before his first arrest, Harold had known he would, one day, be subjected (that's another verbal phrase which, treated differently [and there are several alternative possibilities] would have upset the rolling, flowing prose) to strong scrutiny, likely accompanied by episodes of extreme mental and physical discomfort, (colloquially termed 'torture'), so he developed advanced meditation expertise enabling him to present almost catatonic physiognomic characteristics to would-be inquisitors. (A facility much envied by successful practitioners of the card game poker [and even more envied by the less successful]).

The military guys had soon left him alone. Not so the detectives and insurance investigators. Cops wanted closure on files going back decades. Insurance men were more interested in negotiating deals over pay-outs and –

some hopes – recovery of millions of pounds worth of stolen jewellery.

All this information's stored away in Harold's incredible spongiform mind, along with account numbers, transaction details and balances of confidential accounts in sundry Swiss banks, managed for him by the respectable barrister who (on more than one occasion in the past two decades [albeit both successfully and unsuccessfully]) defended him and Albert.

Albert, after serving seven years of a ten years' sentence, was released to a secure mental institution on the South Downs, where he died insignificantly and alone, at the age of sixty-seven. The proximity of old age had, sadly, engendered unacceptably violent behavioural characteristics, for the inevitable consequences of which the prison authorities wanted to avoid being held responsible.

They felt (with good reason) that they already had to justify enough deaths following the procedure delicately, euphemistically, labelled 'restraint' of healthy young prisoners, suspects and 'troublemakers', without attracting further adverse publicity in restraining nonagenarians. Mental 'facilities' were less likely to attract investigation.

Now therefore, here in 2009, it's time for Harold to set in motion the last act of his dramatic life. He's been planning it for a while. He intends to enjoy it. "We'll have the last laugh", he suggested to still-attractive, ever-loyal Alison as they planned and prepared in the comparative non-privacy of the visitors' room.

(Ismail, alas, is unable further to participate [OR to participate further, depending on your taste in avoidance of split infinitives] in Harold's plans as he was [whether serendipitously, by misadventure or deliberate adversarial mis-direction, was never established] in the US embassy in Beirut on April 18th 1983, when a Chevrolet truck containing some 2000 lbs of explosives …)

*

Through his current solicitor, Harold arranges a visit from the Yard's CID. Duly briefed on the case, a young detective sergeant is shown into the visiting room where Harold awaits.

"Your big chance for promotion, young fellah," he croaks between gasping, heaving coughs. "You take this piece of paper to that address and you'll meet a mathematical genius. You'll have to pay him his fee, of course, then he'll decode this two-thousand-digit number for you. It'll reveal the location of the loot from my last job. (Of course, it does no such thing – it contains instructions to Harold's surviving associates [and successors of those who are no longer surviving] for the accomplishment of his swan song.) Up to you. Do it right and we both win. In no time you'll be a happy DI and I'll be happy to die."

Harold, apparently coughing fit to choke, but actually covering his uncontrollable mirth, signals to be returned to his cell.

Three weeks' searching later, the DS finds only sketchy information on Harold and the unsolved cases. Still-active files lie buried deep in the dust of a rarely visited archive storeroom. The jewellery's never been recovered. He locates the mysterious mathematician; whose fee equals four weeks of the DS's pay. He has trouble getting that okayed by the Super:

"You'd better bring in the loot, laddie, or I'll have that docked from your pay."

A six-figure map reference is provided by the old mathematician (or 'mage' as the simpering DC, clearly a Game of Thrones devotee, calls him/her, it wasn't clear which). Using the full police SATNAV services, they finally arrive at a disused workshop, on a mouldering trading estate, in a suburb of which they've never heard. (For compositional verisimilitude, I should give this tiresome pair names – following the GoT motif I've just introduced, let's call them Hound and Lollys).

They enter, in search of treasure.

In the middle of the concrete floor, apparently swept and vacuumed for the occasion, stands an unmarked wooden packing case, some three feet square. A tentative feel indicates the top's nailed down. Will there really be three million quid's worth of sparklers in there? DC Hound sweats over a borrowed jemmy. His hands tremble as he lifts the lid. It's full of shredded paper. Frantically the pair scatter the packaging far and wide as they delve for the elusive treasure.

Scrabbling hands touch something. Jaws drop. Faces redden. They uncover an eighteen-inches-high plaster cast of a human hand. Clenched, the middle finger points skyward. Angry, frustrated, they drive the two hours back to the prison to demand an explanation from Harold.

One teeth-grindingly, the other nail-bitingly, they wait, impatient. Harold is not brought from his cell. An offhand, bored orderly finally escorts them to the cell. The Governor is already there, standing grim-faced beside a lump of furniture undeserving of the label 'bed'. The Governor's spoiled spaniel enjoys superior sleeping accommodation. The doctor, with her habitual expression of deploring everything about her professional situation, stands beside him, limp hands expressing hopeless defeat, gazing down at the floor next to the un-bed.

Harold's facial expression is not determinable as he is sprawled, face down, on the floor. His solitary death does not appear to have been easy. His hands, one either side of his head, are tight clenched. It's obvious each holds something. Rigor mortis precludes immediate investigation. The silent doctor negatives, with a bitter shake of her head, any attempt to prise those locked fingers open. A team arrives to transport the rigid figure to the morgue.

"You'll just have to wait till the rigor mortis has loosened its grip."

Hours later, the doctor gently prises open the hands.

The Governor, DS Hound, and DC Lollys peer intently.

Each hand clutches a paper twist.

The left holds a world-famous diamond; the right a priceless ruby.

Those present, having watched, only the previous week, the re-run of an earlier BBC Crimewatch programme, have no difficulty in recognising the two fabulous jewels.

The diamond, the Akbar Shah, was once the property of the Mughal emperor Akbar, hence its name. As demonstrated on air, it is engraved on two faces with   inscriptions in Arabic: Shah. Jahan. Malhar Rao Gaekwad of Baroda, India, was the last known owner, though how it came into the possession of the deprived London jeweller, the BBC did not disclose.

The ruby formerly graced the headdress of the Punjabi Maharani Mehtab Kaur, second wife of the ninth and last Maharaja Yadav Indra Singh. (Last, as the Royal line was discontinued on his demise.)

The paper enfolding the diamond says UP

The paper enfolding the ruby says YOURS

Cause of death is duly certified as cardiac arrest due to suffocation resulting from progressive congestion of the lungs and bronchia. Hardly unexpected, but...

"I would have come, if anyone had bothered to call. He must have struggled, in agony to breathe, for hours."

The Governor shrugged.

The police people were interested only in the jewels.

*

Meanwhile, over in Switzerland, there's a jeweller. He's far too discreet to travel to the funeral. From time to time during the succeeding years, he visits various banks, each time leaving deposit boxes less full. He continues to bank cash in sundry numbered accounts from which various charities (including among others, Prisoners' Aid Society, the Prison Education Trust and The Howard League for Prison Reform) have, for decades, been receiving modest anonymous donations.

The value and frequency of these donations will now increase dramatically, in accordance with Harold's pre-mortem instructions. Successive barristers will continue to receive instructions from the Swiss Bank from whom they've been receiving instructions to carry out professional work on prison welfare. Sometimes they prosecute prison malpractice, neglect and corruption where deserved.

And sometimes they win.

(Compliance with Harold's pre-mortem instructions continues to reverberate throughout the hushed and hallowed halls of the British judiciary, even towards the close of the first fifth of the twenty-first century, [which will occur {according to Harold's prediction} at 23.59 hours on the 31st December 2020 and not on the 1st January of that year as some believed on the comparable occasion of the transition from the second to the third millennium AD {or CE if you are that way inclined }]).

*

Lying quietly, relaxed now (how else?), in his open coffin in the Chapel of Rest, hands folded meticulously on his chest, Harold awaits his interment in the shady precincts of the same North London cemetery as many of his former colleagues, prosecutors, persecutors, associates (yes, even victims – after all, in death there can be no distinction [since any decision on dissimilarities of moral-related behaviour falls within the purview of a so-called higher authority]).

Carefully composed on his features (the responsible undertaker's assistant has been faithful to Alison's instructions) is the same gentle, enigmatic smile (a veritable masterpiece of the skilful art of under-taking) that had challenged and frustrated the detectives, the lawyers and the military intelligence officers, many decades earlier. The incredibly nimble, hyperactive brain, enabling-instrument of his career as the most successful (yes, let us by all means acknowledge the intermittent hiccough) jewel thief of his, or any other, century, (in terms of net market value of unrecovered proceeds) no longer carries electrical (or any other) impulses. No longer urges Harold to action.

Alison (reserving her familial right), the last (of many) to pay her respects, bows low over the open coffin. She turns away, briefly raising a hand to the expectant undertaker. He is bemused by the ghost of a Mona Lisa smile…

Without further delay, he steps forward, screws down the lid.

At the reception following the interment, many are puzzled by the gentle, enigmatic smile on the wizened, but still attractive, face of the deceased's ninety-seven-year-old younger sister. Only she will ever know that Harold's hands are no longer folded meticulously on his chest. They lie, palms uppermost, at his sides. But now there is a diamond in his left palm; in the right, a ruby. The jewels are not in paper wraps this time.

*

In due course, a headstone appears on the grave.
                    Rest in Peace, Harold Yardley.
                    Long Live Robin Hood.

*

Afterword: Although Harold's cerebral talents do exist in a few rare cases, his escapades are fictional. However, there really are, regrettably in my opinion, centenarian prisoners serving time in British prisons, with very little in the way of basic medical care, comfort, or support, even in their last days.

*

THE WEARIN' O' THE GREEN

A true tale of the Sport of Kings with a wish-fulfilment ending. Let the reader spot where truth becomes fantasy . . .

Things can happen feckin' fast at thirty miles an hour. As, for example, in the traditionally royal sport of steeplechasing.

Nine beautiful, half-ton quadrupedal equines striving to surmount a series of man-made obstacles and be first to reach a predetermined lateral line across the green, green grass of the course on which they race.

Nine eleven-and-a-half stone bipedal riders competing to persuade their equine partners towards that same objective.

Today, while their mounts stretch tendon and sinew to the full, only seven of the nine jocks will strive for the coveted goal. The other two have murder in mind. Or at least the maximum maiming of one of the seven. Anything can happen …

*

My mother was Romani but her family had given up the travelling life and settled in Berkshire. The touch of the Blarney in me comes through my father's Irish Republican Catholic family. My grandfather ran a small stable. As a child I heard stories of how, when they lived on the Curragh, home of Irish steeplechasing in County Kildare, they would welcome to their house the travelling priests who, it was hinted, at times brought more than the Blessed Sacrament with them.

Troubled times.

Some say everything in the universe, even murder, is a matter of mathematics. The law of retaliation, "An eye for an eye" or "A tooth for a tooth", illustrates the principle that a person who has injured another person is to be penalized to a similar degree, and the person inflicting such punishment should be the injured party.

Then there is the natural law of cause and effect, which means that all our actions have a consequence. At the end of the day we all have to pay a price for the things we do ……

But then again, in Revelations 20:13:
"and each person was judged according to what they had done."

12th March 1924: The Spring Meeting at Cheltenham on a bright but chilly afternoon. At that time, a majority of the stable lads and jockeys in Britain spoke with a strong, almost unintelligible Irish accent. Some were from Ulster, but mostly they were from Eire. A country with too much, too troubled a history of cruelty.

I don't blame the horses, the most noble of beasts.

In the weighing room, minutes before the Gold Cup, Dad is approached by two jockeys – brothers, from the North. Riding against him. They slap his shoulder playfully, just a nice friendly chat – 'and may the best horse win'. Then, the menace … he must *not* win. He opens his mouth –

'Just listen a minute, Charlie. You've already won it twice. Time to give the champion a feckin' chance …'

'No. You listen, boyos. I ride my father's feckin' horses and I ride to feckin' win. You feckin' bully boys aren't goin' to feckin' stop my hat trick. Now get out of my way …'

'Charlie, be reasonable. Remember, anything can happen once you're out there …'

But Dad, green silks shining in the cold sun, is striding away to the parade ring.

The two Ulstermen scowl and shrug.

'His feckin' choice. But if he knows what's good for him …'

They follow him out to where the runners are saddled and ready.

A bell rings.

The paddock steward calls, 'Jockeys mount.'

*

The nine super fit steeplechasers are already on the second circuit, still well bunched. Their steel-shod hooves thunder at thirty miles an hour across the quivering turf of the Gold

Cup course at Cheltenham. *African Night*, the one with my Dad in the plate, is lying third, on the rails; in the early spring sunshine his emerald silks flash among the colourful display. Well lined up and balanced for the fourteenth fence, he knows he can win. Already he can hear the cheering, chanting crowd.

Two horses move up alongside him, one behind the other; too close for comfort; squeezing him tight to the rails. He sees the two jocks, knows instantly what's coming. Before he can react, the front horse, in passing him, swerves to its left, leaving no way through. The second horse, already leaning against Dad's right leg, has him trapped with nowhere to go. Dad strives to hold his line on the rails. The front horse swerves again, its rump colliding with the shoulder of Dad's confused mount. Tossing its head high, it struggles to find somewhere to go. There is nowhere. Simultaneously the second jock slashes his heavy whip twice across Dad's horse's face. It's over in seconds. Terrified, his mount veers away from the vicious onslaught – crashes through the fence wing – scatters shocked spectators… Horrified shouts and screams, the crunch of splintering wood – the distinct crack as a cannon bone snaps. In the stands, the cheering, chanting crowd collectively catches its breath.

The noble horse, Dad's favourite and, today, the bookie's favourite, its foreleg broken beyond mending, its flanks and belly lacerated by the unforgiving shards and splinters, is destroyed by the course vet. The thud of the captive-bolt gun – the 'humane' killer – from behind the makeshift screen, is barely audible to the silent Cheltenham punters. This still happens too often.

An ambulance rushes Dad to Cheltenham hospital. Later to London. His back is broken somewhere in the upper thoracics just below the cervical vertebrae. Though rare, it's one of the worst injuries that can befall a jockey, and it's usually fatal. They mend him – after a fashion – and thereafter, he jokes bitterly, he could audition for Charles Laughton's role – the lead in *The Hunchback of Notre Dame*.

Career over; life and dreams shattered. Never again will he share the thrill, the surge of power in the vibrant, striving muscles as the willing beast beneath him gives its all. The surge of adrenalin coursing through his own veins; the pride and joy each time his father greets him in the winners' enclosure. 'Nice one, Charlie boy.' And never again will I share their pride.

*

Early in 1939, when our elders were making vain efforts to avoid conflict with a certain Adolf Hitler, there appeared one afternoon on the narrow country road outside our house, a gathering of soldiers. In their khaki uniforms they halted their convoy of assorted vehicles, including tracked vehicles they called 'Bren-gun carriers.' All strange to my brothers and me.

At the age of eight, with no political nous, I scarcely understood the cheering, clapping patriotism of my three senior siblings. A neighbour had spread a Union Jack on the hedgerow in front of their house. I suddenly remembered having seen a flag in an upstairs cupboard. Imitating that nationalist impulse, I ran up, threw open the window, and, with the help of my even smaller sister, draped the flag along the sill.

I think it was the commotion among the soldiers outside that drew my mother's attention. She ran outside, followed their angry glares, ran back inside, up the stairs, grabbed the flag, crumpled it up and threw it to the back of the cupboard, scolding me severely.

'You silly boy. You mustn't do that. There'll be trouble'.

Those three words, 'there'll be trouble', summed up a world of inherited oppression and endurance. My honest parents worked hard, but 'the luck of the Irish' passed them by, as it did so many. Mother had struggled all her life, and after the accident, forced to earn what she could, taught primary school.

How was I to know that the splendid standard I'd put out, brilliant in its green, white and orange, was that of the Republic of Ireland?

That story from our childhood sounds funny, doesn't it? But it masked a terrible darkness growing within me. And my sister was my helper . . .

By the end of the war those three older brothers, all of whom were called to military service in the

British forces, were gone. As were Grandad, and our parents. We were alone, in a less innocent world. Sis, three years my junior, proud of her high school education, had become politically aware. Later, like me, she would become politically active...

*

Ezekiel 18:
'Why should not the sons suffer for the iniquity of the father?'

It's nearly six AM, 12th March 1964. Forty years to the day since that disastrous, crippling 'accident'. This morning we've crossed the border and Sis stands in the very Belfast street where my father had rooms when he'd studied Veterinary Science at Queen's University. Until the assassination of Archduke Ferdinand and the ensuing Great War disrupted his dreams.

The day dawns unpleasantly. Early mist hangs heavily over the rooftops as it slowly, miserably drifts across the city. A thin film of fine droplets has settled on the shoulders of her navy serge donkey jacket. The feeble gleam from the late-rising spring sun struggles to illuminate her pale features. Despite the chill that clouds her breath, there's a hint of sweat on her upper lip. People in our line of business know what it means to sweat. And with all our wonderful, world-changing technology, no-one's yet devised the deodorant that can mask the sweet-sour-sweat-smell of tension, of fear.

She stares at the door.

Today she's going in at the sharp end.

Later, when the adrenaline floods through her, her fear will be subsumed, lost in excitement – exhilaration even.

I know what she's thinking. I've been there too many times. This is her first. Right now, she's thinking: 'What am I doing? Was I right to take this on?' Then, more confidently,

'It's not an act of murder, it's an act of war – a private war of retaliation, retribution, *revenge*.'

In her previous job, upper echelon civil servant in the legal department of the Home Office in London, she's watched violent political activists and criminals wriggle free. More than once she's sat in the Central Criminal Court, simmering with frustration as a clever presentation full of legal technicalities has allowed a serious offender, perhaps a known killer, to walk out into the street named Old Bailey EC4, smiling and chatting with his 'associates'. Today's target is one such.

I used to watch her, unseen, from my seat in the press gallery. Could see her fuming. I know things. I get around. My day job is lead crime reporter for one of the London dailies, so no one looks askance when they find me digging in the dirty underworld of crime and racketeering. I don't always report every story I uncover . . .

Couple of years ago, I knew she was ripe and ready. I ensured that she learned all about Dad's 'accident'. I sent in Simms, my recruiter.

She started a new job. Not listed at her local Labour Exchange.

*

I'd hoped to follow Dad and his Dad into racing, but in my teens, my mother mourning him and near her own end, told me the true story of his near-fatal disability, and the death of his favourite horse. That knowledge changed me, set me on a rather different career. Skulking in shadows and dark places; keeping secret surveillance; seeking descendants of the two murderous Ulstermen.

It took two years to trace their war records. Neither made it back from the Second World War. I hoped they suffered.

I discovered each had borne a son, so I set about finding them and when I found them, I discovered each had inherited criminality. Rotten activities were hidden behind their joint 'security' business. Of every kind.

*

My group has no name. No politics. Just a motto:

'IF THE LAW OF THE LAND IS INADEQUATE, THE LAW OF EQUITY DEMANDS AN ALTERNATIVE'.

Sis – no names, no pack drill – is slim, stylish, sophisticated, carrying herself with poised and athletic assurance. She has the family features, as do I. Raven-black hair, swept back in two wings above glittering jet eyes ringed with ashy kohl. In my terms she's well trained, efficient, resourceful – and dedicated. Single, cold-eyed, but not cold-hearted. You need a warm heart to punish injustice. In the two years since she joined us, she's done eight jobs. Serious, violent jobs. Serious, but never *extreme*. Natural justice.

Sis and I no longer lived imaginatively in the 'sport of kings' world of horses. What the rest of the family would have made of our lives, I never asked myself, nor I suspect, did she.

A gathering of ravens is called a 'conspiracy'. In some cultures, like the ancient Irish, the raven was revered as a godlike creature. A carrion bird, eating the dead, ravens became associated with lost souls, ghosts of murdered people denied Christian burial, even – the damned. Culturally, the raven symbolises the dark side; hate, aggression – revenge.

Natural science, on the other hand, now considers them to be among the world's most intelligent animals, with a high encephalization quotient, and a distinct love of play. Among other skills are episodic memory and the ability to use individual experience in predicting the behaviour of others.

I said our group has no name, true enough. But we thought of her as –

Ravenheart.

My twentieth century *Raven* has made her mark. In the annals of Eire's cruel history, she's a legend. Those who haven't, hope never to meet her. Knee cappings had come as an even more shocking surprise at the hand of a smiling, coquettish, pistol packing colleen – the wraith who is my kid sister.

Killing? No! I've never given her a Termination, a solo job. It takes something extra to cross that line. Our targets inhabit society's political stratosphere as well as its criminal underbelly. Danger was the air we breathed.

Some jobs I do. Others, I ask for a volunteer from my specialist team. Finding the target, usually a *him*, alone is rarely possible, requiring coordinated teamwork to isolate them.

Throughout these two years I've groomed her for this.

Today, for the first time, she's part of a Termination team. Today, her training'll pay off. Today, Sis will play her role in an act of extreme violence.

She's currently an employee of the cleaning company contracted for the two-storey building she now contemplates from across the dingy Belfast backstreet. The Target operates from his 'office suite' on the ground floor of this undistinguished redbrick house with its politically challenging mural painted on the gable end. A front for crime.

She first cleaned these offices three weeks ago, when the regular cleaner called in sick. (Currently enjoying an expenses-paid holiday in the Canaries).

In her shamrock green coverall, she's in there every Monday to Friday, so she is. Today will be her last, she reflects grimly.

Parked twenty yards to her left is a Belfast City Council Department of Sanitation truck. We've ensured there's been intermittent trouble with a blocked sewer over the past twenty-four hours.

She glances at the truck; back to the door. Touches the watch on her wrist.

The LED on my Detector blinks. My Sewage Gas Detector.

Bold and confident now, she crosses the street. Presses the CALL button. Inside a buzzer sounds. The woman monitoring the CCTV checks the screens. The door latch clicks.

Sis walks in, just as she's done on fifteen of the last twenty-one days. Passes through the metal detector. The lean, mean-looking bottle blonde in her shabby grey suit, slight bulge to the left of her left breast, greets her coolly. Pats her down. Escorts her everywhere as she works calmly, wordlessly, for the next three-and-a-half hours.

In her head she's humming *For the Wearin' o' the Green / For the wearin' o' the green. / They're hangin' men and women / For the wearin' o' the green.*

An Irish street song dating back to before the 1798 Rebellion, when wearing the green was an act of defiance punishable by hanging. It meant war.

She's just finishing up the Ground Floor.

The Target's not a big man. Like me, he hasn't followed in his jockey father's footsteps. I know him and his cousin intimately, though we've never met. Major gang leader, into the dirty stuff, kiddie porn and trafficking being his speciality. His gang handle the 'goods', brought in from Eastern Europe. His cousin looks after the money laundering. We know where to find him, too. Naturally.

The Target's a man of habit. His biological clock demands that he leave his desk daily – an hour after breakfasting. At nine-thirty-three, he leaves his office. Nods as he passes his nameless cleaner and her chaperone in the hallway.

"Top o' the mornin' to ye, girls."

Goes into the Men's room at the rear of the building. A Men's room with a single lockable stall.

Time for Sis to leave. Finishing her dusting, she again presses a button on her wristwatch, gathers the tools of her trade and carries them to the cupboard near the front door, opens it, grabs her jacket, and leaves. The blonde, sole occupant of the building beside the target, will, she knows, follow her straight outside, ostensibly for a smoke. We never, ever, permit 'collateral damage'.

In the Sanitation Department vehicle, the 'Muck Truck' we call it, an LED is flashing Green. The three of us glance at each other, nod.

Green means GO.

My colleagues exit the truck and collect our remaining tools. They replace the manhole cover, all the time aware of the guard smoking, Ravenheart walking away down the street. Their hands are never far from their concealed weapons.

The waterproof plastic explosive device is the size of a breakfast sausage, of similar appearance and texture. Or, put it another way, turd-shaped. We introduced it into the sewage system yesterday.

The flashing green light means the Target's in position, sitting, presumably comfortably, right where I want him.

I press the red button next to the flashing LED on my Sewage Gas Detector. The device negotiates the remaining yard and a half of its subterranean voyage. My monitor screen shows it's exactly in position under the Ground Floor WC.

Orange button.

It's primed.

Green button…

Taking advantage of the instant chaos, the Muck Truck is already moving as Sis and the lads climb aboard.

'How did I do, Big Bro?'

High fives all round.

'Sure, ye've done a grand job, Sis. One down, one to go.'

Ravens, whose love of play shows their exceptional intelligence, are also associated with revenge … and death ...

THE WEARIN' O' THE GREEN

O Paddy dear, and did ye hear the news
that's goin' round?
The shamrock is by law forbid to grow on Irish
ground!
Saint Patrick's Day no more we'll keep, his
colours can't be seen
For they're hangin' men and women for
the wearin' o' the green.

I met with Napper Tandy, and he took me by the
hand,
He said, How's dear old Ireland, and how does
she stand?
She's the most distressful country that you have
ever seen,
For they're hangin' men and women for
the wearin' o' the green.

For the wearin' o' the green

For the wearin' o' the green
They're hangin' men and women for the wearin'
o' the green.

Then since the colour we must wear is England's
cruel red
Sure Ireland's sons will ne'er forget the blood
that they have shed
You may take the shamrock from your hat, and
cast it on the sod
But 'twill take root and flourish there tho'
underfoot 'tis trod.

My father loved his country and sleeps within its
breast,
While I that would have died for her must never
so be blessed.
Those tears my mother shed for me, how bitter
they'd have been
If I had proved a traitor to the wearin' o' the
green.

For the wearin' o' the green
For the wearin' o' the green
They're hangin' men and women for the wearin'
o' the green.

But if, at last, her colours should be torn from
Ireland's heart

Her sons, with shame and sorrow, from the dear
old isle will part.
I've heard a whisper of a land that lies beyond
the sea,
Where rich and poor stand equal in the light of
freedom's day.

Oh Ireland must we leave you driven by a
tyrant's hand
And seek a mother's blessing from a strange and
distant land,
Where the cruel cross of England shall never
more be seen
And in that land we'll live and die, still wearing
Ireland's green.

For the wearin' o' the green
For the wearin' o' the green
They're hanging men and women for the wearin'
o' the green.

It was sung to the tune similar to "Yellow Rose of Texas" and has been
recorded many times, on both sides of the Atlantic.

*

MEET MRS INGRAM

A story of Sex Spies Skis & Sports Cars

Part 1

Christmas in Clapton

It all started that Christmas, when she was eleven years old. She lived in a poor area on the east side of London, north of the Thames. 'Supermac' was Prime Minister. He'd told the nation they'd 'never had it so good.' She could remember the bitterness in their voices when her Mummy and Daddy had read that in the paper.

It hadn't been much of a party. It never was. Just Mummy and Daddy. Her Mummy did her best. There were no illusions about a red-suited Santa with a sack of goodies. She knew better than to expect toys on a tree; balloons and baubles, paper hats and presents. She went to bed early; at least that way she could keep warm. Snuggled down to sleep.

Her Daddy came quietly into the room and sat on the edge of her bed. He'd stopped doing that some years back. She looked at him, wondering what…and why… He reached out for her hand.

"You know we couldn't give you much in presents, Blossom, so now you've started swimming lessons at school, I wonder if you'd like to go to the pool one evening a week and learn to dive. I'll come with you at first and look after you."

She knew swimming and diving had been her Daddy's unattainable childhood ambitions. Two World Wars and the Great Depression had only made the poor poorer. They'd talked about it before, but she wasn't expecting this. She knew there was very little money coming in each week since her Daddy's accident at the Tilbury Docks where he'd worked. She didn't understand it all, but she knew things were bad.

Municipal pools were few and far between in the less privileged London Boroughs. Jumping in three at a time made a super splash and was a lot of fun. The chance to learn to dive seemed too good to believe. She sat up and hugged her Daddy; saw the tears in his eyes, too. Wow! Some Christmas present!

She went back to school in the New Year determined to do her best at her lessons as well as the swimming and diving. Daddy was going to be proud of his little Blossom. She saw his pleasure when she moved up each level of the diving boards. Soon, he was goading her to the three-metre board, highest of the high boards at her local pool. Then he would beam with delight as, with eyes tight shut and knots in her stomach, she tried to live out that dream for him. In no time at all, she discovered the thrilling, free-fall sensation of the high-dive. Found herself wishing there could be an even higher board. Wondered, with butterflies in her stomach, if she would be able to face ten metres, like the Olympics. She was hooked.

Music and reading were her favourite pastimes. There was no electricity in their house, just gas lights. The wireless worked on a wet 'accumulator' that had to go to the garage every week or two, to be re-charged. 'BBC Third Programme' it was called. Her favourites were Beethoven and Mozart, though many of the others pleased her too.

Her only other present that Christmas Day was a battered, much-used fairy-cycle. The free library was at the bottom of the hill where she lived. The brakes didn't work - the thrill of speed was born. It was worth the walk back up, pushing her cycle and carrying her precious library book. Sometimes she would start reading the book before she left the library, only realising she had walked home without her fairy cycle when it was too late.

After leaving school with a good School Certificate, she drifted through several dead-end jobs. Small supermarkets were popping up in the various shopping centres but they didn't pay much for cleaners, or shelf-stackers or even check-out staff. After giving her Mummy money for her keep, there wasn't much left of her meagre wages for her own pursuits. All through her 'teens, she day-dreamed about those thrills back in her schooldays. Thrills that faded into treasured memories.

In her late twenties, she was good-looking rather than beautiful, with athletic grace and body strength from all her training for the swimming and diving. She got a steady job in a turkey-packing factory. She had worn her dark hair in a short bob; easier to tuck under the swimming cap. Health regulations at the factory decreed the hair must be covered so she felt no need to grow it longer. Awfully smelly things, turkeys; not much fun.

Minimum wage, but some good work-mates. Especially the Polish immigrant girls. Their parties were fun and she learned to share their taste for vodka. They always brought some back from their summer trips home. Mixed with lime and mint, it made a super mojito. She had to be careful not to drink too many and get tipsy. She had a short-lived affair with Leonard, one of the young trainee managers. Discovered she was more interested in his sports car than his bed. After a few weeks, he left to take a job with a competitor.

David, driver of the big, red, London Transport double-decker that took her to work each day, asked her for a date. As romances went, it was no big deal. More and more people started eating more and more turkeys. They made her a Quality Assessor and Poultry Welfare Officer. Raised her pay. Responsible for all those thousands of limp, smelly carcases every day.

David proposed. Life went on…

``````````````````````````````````````````````````

She misses the thrills of her childhood. The brief moment between leaving the high board and cleaving the water. Hurtling dangerously down the hill to change her library book. More recently, those few weeks sharing Leonard's sports car – and his bed. She still loves her books and the magic of music. She puts the mojito on her bedside table; next to the vodka bottle. David's snoring, like everything else about him, is gentle and un-disturbing. Picks up her bed-time read. Ian Fleming's latest.

He can transport her to an exciting, different, make-believe world. A world of sex, spies, sports cars, skiing! She's never thought much of sex. And there has been a rumour that Leonard, briefly her lover, was an industrial spy. She can't think why anyone would want to spy on a lot of dead turkeys. As for speed and sports cars, well, her David certainly knows how to handle his fifteen tons of gleaming red, double-decker bus. But oh, how she would
``````````````````````````````````````````````````

love the chance to glide and swoop down a snow-covered Alpine mountain.

Christmas is always the busiest time of year, keeping all the big supermarket chains stocked up. The live turkeys come in from the farms each day, thousands in each huge lorry. They go out the same day, plucked, trussed, wrapped and refrigerated.

It's been a heavy day at the factory; three shifts a day for about six weeks. She turns to her bookmarked page, eager to catch up with Commander Bond on his latest mission. 007's spectacular skiing as he soars over the railway, thrilling as it is, can't do it. Eyelids droop…chin drops on her chest…spectacles slip from her nose…glass from her fingers…book to the floor…

Part
2
Cataclysm in Cambridge

She blunders blindly out of bed. Kills the alarm. Stands, yawns, stretches to her full five-feet-five; flexes, farts, crotch-scratches. In that order. Yesterday's memories come oozing woozily back into her tired brain.

*Oh, yes. Today is the end of my first week as a trainee spy. Whoops! Mustn't say 'spy' anymore. Mustn't even think 'spy'. Not ever again. I am a trainee **C**ounter **I**ntelligence **A**gency **O**perative.*

She says it out loud, trying to convince herself. She looks in the pier glass.

Too much bosom and bum to be a Mata Hari. Don't fancy facing a firing squad, either.

She's looked it up on Google.

Too short for a dancer. Or a Bond girl. Muscles in all the wrong places, too.

Her job as head of security with an international supermarket chain is behind her now.

*Next week, I'll start at the **P**reliminary **T**raining **F**acilities **E**stablishment. Training Division Four. **PTFE.***

TD4. *Well, that's what the guys call it. They seem to think there's some screwy motoring joke in it somewhere. Stupid acronyms.*

She struggles with the zip on her smart, new, black jump-suit.

Better be careful. Can't do with Robertson's Silver Shred smeared down the front.

She fondles admiringly, proudly, the logo above her left breast.

In silver letters all intertwined and surrounded by a laurel wreath with a crown over the top.

For six whole months. Shouldn't be too difficult.

Flexes her shoulders at the thought.

They seem to think me well qualified. Karate black belt. Archery. Pistol shooting. I only just missed qualifying for the British team last year. They know about my sky-diving stunts, too.

She's immodestly let it drop that she's driven David's Porsche a few laps round Silverstone.

David had gone missing for a few days last year, while on a mission. That's when they'd recruited her. Someone from *CIAO PTFE TD4,* a stranger in a long, black, Sydney Greenstreet overcoat, black Homburg hat, rimless glasses, bristly mouse-coloured moustache (and a cringing speech defect she couldn't miss) (oh, and a black leather briefcase) had rung her door bell.

"I'm afwaid yaw husband has disappeahed, Mrs Ingwam. We know, fwom David, befaw he went to gwound, that you possess certain qualifications don't you know. He'd talked about it with us. Wobertshaw and me, that is. Wobertshaw's my boss, d'you know. David's too. Oh, but you don't know, do you."

The bristly moustache twitched, like a nervous mouse, with each mangled 'r'.

"We know maw about yaw husband than you do Mrs Ingwam, but we think you might be best qualified to look faw him faw us. You see, we know quite a lot about you, too. No, please."

The mouse had rested. He'd raised a deprecatory, black-gloved hand. Winter had not yet surrendered to the sweet, subverting, trilling syllables of an eager spring song.

"We thought David might have explained things maw to you."

``````````````````````````````````
``````````````````````````````````

David hadn't been happy when she'd told him the **Agency** wanted her. They wouldn't be working together. The **Agency** didn't allow it. Not husband and wife. She smiles as she thinks of the guys in her class. She's seen one or two looking her way.

Don't be silly. They don't allow that, either. Pity David's away. I do miss him when he's away working…

She sets the coffee to perk. Butter and Robertson's on the table. Two slices of wholegrain into the toaster. Makings for her first spliff on the table ready for later.

So convenient, growing their own, up on the bin floor above the flat. Opens the French doors. Steps out onto the balcony. Stretches; breathing the fresh, early-morning air. She loves the semi-isolation of the old corn mill they've had converted. The sails had already rotted beyond salvation when they'd bought it. Removing the remnants had enabled the balcony to encircle the fourth-floor. From where she stands, she can see for miles across the flat landscape of the fens. She faces towards the spires of Ely Cathedral. Cathedrals and other great churches hold a special fascination in the minds of many people. For her, Ely, standing on a slight rise in the ground away to the north, was no exception. Walking half-way round she can see Cambridge, only minutes away in the Porsche.

Those heavy, grey clouds probably carry rain or even snow.

She glances down to where her own latest toy stands. 1967 Austin Healey. Ex-competition car, damaged while racing on the Sebring track in America. The late owner-driver wasn't going to need it again. David had bought it and had it rebuilt. 3000 Mark III, one of the last built in 1967. High-lift camshaft. HD SU8 carburettors. He'd had it finished in brilliant, metallic scarlet.

No petrolhead, she doesn't actually know a camshaft from a carburettor. David always looks after all that. Just loves driving it though. Twenty-fifth birthday present from David. Lovely surprise when he'd taken her to collect it from the garage in Cambridge last year. Older than she is, by a long way. "Twice your age and twice as beautiful" he'd quipped. Blushed when he'd realised his gaffe. He'd put his arm round her, trying to laugh it off.

Toaster pops. She turns to go in – pauses, mid-stride.
What on earth is that bundle down by the dustbins? I'm sure it wasn't there last night when I got home. Oh, I'll take a look later. Hang on! It's wearing David's tartan windcheater. **Shiiit! It can't be.**

She doesn't know whether to faint or vomit, or both.
Come on girl. Make the Agency proud of you. Keep Calm and Carry On…Bugger that. If that's David…

She's half way down the spiral staircase, gasping for breath against the convulsive contractions of her diaphragm, when she remembers she hasn't picked up her phone.
If that's David down there…
From the fourth floor, she hadn't been sure.
…I'll need more than my phone. If it isn't, I'm going to feel such a fool. No. Keep going. Make sure first.

She hits the ground, running. At the back door, she

……

Bugger again. The keys are with my phone on the table.

Tries to see from the window.

Shit. Obscure glass. What do I do?

She stretches to see through the peep-hole in the bleached oak door. Can see the Healey but not the bins.

Four flaming floors.

Reaches the third-floor landing; just has to stop for breath. Leans over the handrail, whole body heaving and sobbing. Remembers David's words last night. "I'll be putting some old clothes out for the re-cycling truck in the morning darling, and I'll be leaving early," he'd whispered, as they'd snuggled down to sleep. And then, this morning. "See you in a week or two. Don't worry," he'd called, as he closed the back door.

What a thoughtless thing to say. Of course I'll worry. For better, for worse, I love the guy.

She lets herself collapse, sliding down until she sits, breathing heavily, against the curve of the bleached oak bannisters.

How could I be so utterly stupid? His old clothes. Of course.

Hauling herself upright, she plods up the final flight, back into the kitchen. Toast's cold; coffee's luke-warm. She feels shattered. Starts over. Fresh coffee. Fresh wholegrain. Sits hunched over her delayed breakfast. Feels helpless and useless

Stupid aspiring spy. Yeah. I should cocoa.

She shoots bolt upright, second cup of coffee scalding her thighs.

Stupid, stupid, stupid! If David put old clothes out, he'd've put them in a bin-liner. He wouldn't just throw them out rolled up in a bundle. **Wrapped up in his windcheater.**

She turns at the door to grab phone and keys from the table, before hurtling recklessly down the death-spiral for the second time. Fingers fumbling frantically, she thrusts in the key.

Anti-clockwise, fool. Aah. It won't turn. No, you blithering idiot. It's not even locked. **Not locked…!**

Trips over the steps as she staggers to the dustbins. Chest still heaving from her exertions, she leans over the bundle.

Daaaviiid!

Her scream chokes into vomit. Minutes later, she climbs to her feet, straightens her dishevelled clothes, takes three deep breaths and chides herself,

You're an accredited, trainee, Counter Intelligence Agency Operative. **'Remain calm and controlled at all times.' 'Behave with dignity and restraint, especially when dealing with an emergency.'**

She admires her calmness, dignity, and restraint, as her fingers fumble frantically again. Remembers how to work the speed-dial facility they've taught her to use on her new phone. Her tutor answers instantly. Calmly and rationally, she explains.

Yes, of course I'm sure it's David. Yes, of course I'm sure he's dead. Yes, of course I'm sure he wasn't there last night – **I'd have noticed. No, I don't effing know how he effing got there. He didn't effing walk there and lie down and effing die, did he? Somebody's …"**

Her scream sounds hoarse in her ears.

I've missed my train. I'll be late for class. I promised to phone Daddy this morning.
I haven't fed Tiddles. And David's…

She tries to listen to her tutor. "Not a matter for **PTFE. TD4**. You'll have to ring Robertshaw in Cologne. No, no. Not Robertson – Robertshaw. He's David's line manager."

He gives her the number. She puts it straight into her phone.

"And don't call the police, Mrs Ingram, whatever you do. And don't move him, will you. Robertshaw will know what to do. You must do exactly as Robertshaw tells you.

"You must follow procedures. Trust Robertshaw. Stout fellah. Grand chap. Pukka Sahib. One of our very best. Yes, yes, and good luck. I'm so sorry about your husband, Mrs Ingram. Yes, yes. Occupational hazard, don't you know. No, don't bother coming to class today."

I'll have to ask David about Pukka Saab. I've heard Uncle George say it, but he drives an E-type. Perhaps it's not important. I hope Robertshaw lives up to the hype.

Scrambles into the Healey. She took it to Europe last year, on a holiday trip.

Accepts it's no match for David's Porsche Cayman S. Glances round the yard.

Where is his Porsche, anyway? This trip'll be no holiday. No, don't bother packing anything. You've got all you'll need in your shoulder-bag in the boot.

Remembers she hasn't fed the cat.

Poor old Tiddles'll have to fend for himself. There's plenty of mice and rats and...whatever cats eat, around the mill. Whoa! Not so fast. I should ring Robertshaw first.

Speed-dials again. 'Robertshaw's personal phone,' her tutor had said.

"Yes, yes, Mrs Ingram. G-get here as s-soon as you c-can. No, no It's imp-p-portant you come in your lovely r-red c-car. Q-quicker than pah-public tuh-transport. Yes, leave things egg-exactly as they are at y-your p-place. D-don't touch anything. I'll have someone there in no time. No, no. Don't ring the police. I'll have someone cah-clear up the m-mess ah d-deal with th-the situation."

He gives her the Cologne address. She logs it in the satnav.

Once I clear Cambridge and hit the M11 it should be child's play to Dover. Expect the M25'll be its usual bloody morning mess. Round to the M20. Piece of cake. Re-fuel in Dover or Calais, depending on ferry time. Don't know the second leg at all. Autoroute link at Calais looks easy enough. East onto the E40. Yeah. Trust satnav and go for it. With luck, I'll make it in a bit over seven hours and just arrive in daylight.

Her eyes slide past the dustbins as she thumbs the starter. Checks the gauges. Prays it won't rain – or snow. Once outside the gate, she balances clutch and accelerator. No burned rubber – just as David has taught her…Well short of Aachen, she pulls into the filling station, as per satnav.

That's a Porsche; silver; like David's; over on the parking area. So what? Plenty of them about on these fast roads. Better get back out there again.

Onto the exit road. Checks her mirrors.

Oh! There's the Porsche pulling out as well.

She accelerates away, shifting easily through the gears. Hits the ton and doesn't lift her foot. Checks the gauges again. Rear view mirror? The Porsche is way back. Ten minutes later she notices it, right up her tail. She can read the plate.

*"Good God. **It is David's**. What the hell's going on?"*

Feels the warm dampness of her…Presses harder on the loud pedal.

*120 - 123 – 124 – 5 - 6 – 127. That's it. Audrey, the Austin Healey's giving her best. **Shit!** Where did they come from?*

Two black Mercedes AMGs and two motor cycles have popped out from behind the Porsche. Spread across the two lanes but hanging back. The Porsche is glued to her bumper. Motor cycles look like police. No panic now. She's in her element. One of her elements. Slip road and fly-over coming up. Unreadable road sign on the gantry flashes past.

Time for evasive action.

Only metres from the slip road, she jams the wheel quarter turn hard right. Then even harder left. Shrieking tyres leave smoking black rubber behind as she fishtails into the junction.

Chicane? Hah! Piece of cake. Dear, dead David taught me well.

She clears the roundabout at the top of the rise. Silver Porsche and two black Mercs nearly half a mile away. Haven't even slowed.

No way they'll be doin' a U-ie.

At the bottom of the slip road she would have to take to re-join the autoroute, are two, black-clad motor cyclists. Can't see faces through the visors.

Surely I saw them as I was joining the autoroute in Calais. Surely not. Those would have been French. Can't make these out. They must be working in relays; **escorting me! They must think I'm pretty important!** *France – Belgium. What about Germany? And I've been ignoring speed restrictions all the way.*

For nearly a minute she just sits, letting the adrenalin-shakes settle. An arm waves, beckoning her down. She rolls slowly forward, unsure what to expect. One of the riders pulls out onto the carriageway. The other waves her on; tucks in behind her. She lets the lead rider control their speed all the way across the border and into Cologne. He doesn't hang about either. Never sees David's silver Porsche again. Or the black Mercs. As they forge through the suburbs, the motor-cycles blend and merge into the city traffic but that's no problem.

Whoopee! Satnav rules!

At the top of the hill, she passes Robertshaw's house and parks in a side-street. Her knickers are still damp. Her hands still shaky.

Whew! I'm here. CIAO, Cologne!

*

Part 3
Confabulation in Cologne

Her whole body trembles with a frisson of excitement. She clenches her abs and glutes.

Of course it isn't fear.

She stands at the top of the long, steep street. Looks down on the celebrated cathedral spire. Early evening mist begins to rise over the famous river. Ahead of her the feeble gleam from the soon-to-set sun struggles to illuminate her features. Behind her a waning moon shines dully as it rises over the city's mist-shrouded roof tops. An eerie atmosphere of half-light and shadows. Unbidden, her mind recalls the grim scene she left behind at the mill. Despite the chill that clouds her breath, perspiration films her upper lip. People in her line of business know what it means to sweat, and there is no deodorant that can mask the sweet-sour-sweat-smell of fear. She stares at the door.

When this is over, I'm going to count those five-hundred-and thirty-three steps for myself.

Late afternoon commuter traffic crawls across one of the many bridges spanning the Rhine. She steps behind a convenient laurel bush. Feels stupid and a bit scared. Stares again at the door opposite.

Hope to God it's the right one.

The low, autumn sun barely warms her back, doing nothing for the cold chill that clutches the pound of lead where her pounding heart used to be.

What am I doing? Was I right to come? Bristly Moustache said only in an emergency. What the hell? This is an emergency! That's my David. Dead among the dirty damned dustbins. You bet it's a flaming emergency! It's an escalating epidemic of erupting emergencies! I've come so far. Perhaps I should have rung. Oh, no. He said not to. Wire taps or something.

Her panicking mind flies off into wild scenes of the torture rooms the guys in class joke about. Buried deep in the infamous cellars of Lubjanka. Her racing heart eases back into overdrive.

*Cruisin' gal. Cruisin'. Suppose he's not in. I could stand here for days. No, you couldn't, stupid. Someone would see you and... Perhaps he has someone else in there. Another **O**perative and we're not supposed to meet? No. I'd know. He'd've told me. How the hell did I get involved in this? I'm not trained for it. Field work, they call it. Dammit, I haven't even **seen** the **P**reliminary **T**raining **F**acilities **E**stablishment yet. Six months minimum, they said, before I'd leave the first place and then another six somewhere else. Then out working alongside an experienced field operative. Hell's effing bells. I knew David's work was dodgy before we married.*

Should've known it couldn't work. I don't even know whether Robertshaw's in there. I bet it's not his real name anyway. As if it matters now. He can't just sit in there waiting for some shit-scared sucker to come knocking at his door because her stupid secret agent of a husband has got himself killed and dumped in his own backyard. Only half-hidden by the bloody bins, too. Whoever put him there meant me to see him as soon as I opened the backdoor this morning. I really must stop thinking this way.

She shrugs, to dispel the uninvited images.

I've come all this way; I can't run away now. Cambridge to Cologne by public transport? What do they think I am? In the Healey, it took me just under seven hours. With a police escort! All the way, for all I know.

She feels the simmering anger come rising to the boil again, as she remembers Bristly Moustache's first visit.

A right load of old codswallop he dished out. The silly shit. They'd 've done a security check on me before they let things go too far between David and me. Probably knew where I buy my panties. Hehehe."

She giggles convulsively as she remembers David joking, they even knew her favourite condom colour.

'Course they knew all about me. Martial arts with David and stuff like that. Archery and the gun club. Hell, it was only .22 pistol stuff. Indoors. Did they think that'd made me some sort of heroine-in-waiting? Just because I did that crazy skydiving twice a week for an advert they all thought I must be brave and daring.

She's never told anyone, not even David, she'd made up a tune for the jingle.

"I go up in an aeroplane.

I jump when it's time to come down again.

Twice a week I pee my pants,

At fifteen thousand feet."

Which can be difficult when you're strapped up tight in that bloody harness.

She giggles again.

It paid well though. Like the diving, it was only to please Daddy at first. This is different! This is for real! They play for flaming keeps, this lot! I'd grown up a bit when I met David at the gym.

He seemed just a nice, normal, ordinary sort of guy. Nothing secretive about him. He didn't tell me anything until we were in bed together that first time. It was only squash and badminton and the gym at first. But it was still only for fun. The fun of winning. Beating some of those self-opinionated prats who pranced and preened around the club bars. I suppose I let him lead me on. 'The more grown-up stuff' he called it.

That time he'd been late reporting in, he'd turned up none the worse after about ten days. They'd got their hooks into her by then and persuaded her.

"You've got what it takes Mrs Ingwam. We can make a weally excellent opewative out of you, don't you know."

With an effort she drags her mind back to the present. The Victorian house across the road. Robertshaw somewhere inside. She hopes. Recent images replay across her mind, distracting her attention.

That was David's body lying outside the back door!

She'd jumped in the Healey and driven away from...She's back at screaming pitch.

I wonder if it's still there. **Oh, my God. The binmen come tomorrow. They won't take him away with the... Will they?**

She feels the panic rising again.

Is somebody watching me from behind those upstairs curtains?

Tries not to look as if she's looking.

Silly me. CCTV these days. Is my hair tidy? Stop rambling, idiot.

Gathering her wits, she makes sure no-one's looking her way. With a toss of her head, she steps from behind the laurel bush. In the fast fading light she strides, like an Operative on a Mission, across the street. Hopes she looks bold and confident, even if there is only a camera watching. Steps up to the door. Dark blue gloss, recently painted.

Look, there's a run. Just there.

Polished brass bell-pull. Pulls her sleeve down to cover her hand. Yanks at it, daring him not to be in. She hadn't met Robertshaw last time. Bristly Moustache had come to Cambridge to see her. She listens, her hopes sinking as the deep clangs fade away.

Stop there, gal. Take a breath and try again. If it comes to the worst, you can wait until he comes back. If he comes back... If somebody hasn't terminated him as well. Silly bloody word, terminated. Killing's killing and dead's dead. **Like David's effing dead. Half hidden behind the flaming bins.**

She clenches her teeth to stop the scream escaping.

What if Wobertsh... aahhh... Robertshaw's not answering 'cos he's lying out in his back garden? Won't be a back yard in a street like this. Anonymous among the antirrhinums. Concealed by the chrysanthemums. Hidden in the hollyhocks. Inanimate amid the irises. Masked by the Michaelmas daisies. Prone among the periwinkles. Terminated next to the Tiger Lilies... ...or whatever secret agents grow in their back gardens in the smarter suburbs of Cologne.

She feels another scream coming on.

Stop it. You're getting hysterical.

She pulls the bell again, though there's little hope left in her heart.

Shit! I forgot to pull my sleeve...

Waits again as the bell repeats its clangour.

'Somewhere, deep in the bowels of the three-storey Victorian villa, a bell tolled... slowly... mournfully...' 'and therefore never send to know for whom the bells tolls; it tolls for thee.' 'The curfew tolls the knell of parting day...' Jesus, where did I read that? I've waited long enough.

She turns to walk away. Jumps! as the latch clicks behind her. Suddenly, there he is. Shirtless. Bare-foot. For her, the moment is electric, like the build-up to a storm.

Apart from David, he is her first **real** spy. His stooping torso, straggly, greying chest-hair and droopy man-boobs; sagging shoulders, spindly arms, arthritically deformed feet...

'Stout fellah. Pukka Saab. One of our best,' her tutor had said on the phone. Seconds pass...as she stares, aghast.

*What's this ageing, stooped husk of a man doing about my David? David, lying there stone cold – stone dead dammit? Curled around one of the dustbins, hugging it, like he was hump... **Where the f—k's 007?"** This can't be Robertshaw. Must be his butler.*

The coolness of the gloomy interior calms her confused mind. She clenches her near-chattering teeth. Squeezes out her rehearsed conversation-opener.

Good afternoon. I've called to see Mr W-aah – Robertshaw. Is he available please? He is expecting me.

The hysteria isn't far away. Again. She nearly giggles at the ridiculous scene.

I've never seen a bare-chested butler before. Butlers don't answer the door shirtless and shoeless. And braces! Ye gods. Not in polite, English society. I really thought Germany was much like England in most respects.

The walking cadaver stoops even lower, holds the door wide for her. He stretches out a claw of a hand attached to its pink, stick-like arm.

"Gah-Good day to you Mrs Ingram. I am expecting you. Won't you pah- please come in."

His voice is weak, as though it takes a lot of effort to enunciate. Enunciate? Did I mean 'enunciate?' or 'articulate?'

She shakes her head in disbelief and his hand in greeting.

Gently, *stupid. You might pull it off. A spy with one arm isn't going to be any flaming use to you. Or David. David! Oh God. What did they do to him? How did they termin…?*

The back-yard vision rises again. Hysteria is imminent. Her hand flies to her mouth.

Her teeth hurt her knuckles more than her knuckles hurt her teeth.

"Actually, I was n-not expecting you q-quite so s-soon, my dear. Hence my pah-present, wholly inadequate and uh-unsuitable attire. For which p-please accept my most ah-abject apologies. I was in the sh-shower d'you see. Showers are so much more s-sah-civilised and hygienic, don't you think. I take it you shah-shower, you know – when you ah…"

Good God, two of them at it! Is it in MI6's job description? 'Mild speech impediment an advantage.'

His voice has tailed off. She's caught no trace of embarrassment in either tone or manner. He turns to lead her across the travertine-tiled hall into a spacious drawing-room with high, Victorian cornices. Floor to ceiling drapes.

What the…?

She hasn't seen an aspidistra in years.

"Please Mrs Ingram, won't you sah-sit down while I-ah-ah-...?" He gestures with one of the flesh-coloured sticks. His demeanour jaunty, he strides across the richly coloured, contoured carpet into an adjoining room. When he reappears, minutes later, his smart business suit is dark, charcoal-grey. A brilliant red carnation completes the transformation. Following him into the room limps the man with the rimless glasses and bristly moustache (and speech impediment.) He carries the black Sydney Greenstreet top-coat over one arm; the black Homburg hanging from his other hand.

Funny. He wasn't limping when he came to see me in Cambridge. I wonder if he had anything to do with...

The magnificent, carnation-red drapes respond to the press of a button. Smoothly, silently they shut out the gloomy, grey clouds that creep across the vibrant glow of the approaching sunset. Interior illumination, it seems, has responded to the same button. She tries to look casual and relaxed as she drops her shoulder-bag on the floor beside the easy chair. Sits transfixed in puzzlement.

Is it the same man? It's the same face but he's changed bodies. He can't have. It must all be part of the stupid games they play. Fools anyone watching when he appears at the door, I suppose. Fooled me. And I'm supposed to be clever enough to be a sp.... Whoops.

Wob-Robertshaw, if that's his name, turns from the smart, modern cocktail bar opposite the window.

"You see, Mrs Ingram, your hah-husband, ah your late hu-husband that is, had been tah-turned by ah the others. He had become what we call ah a d-d- double agent. We were aware of this, of course and were taking suh-suitable precautions. You see D-David had tuh-taken improper pup-possession of some documents that he intended to tah-take with him and not come back. You may recall he mum-made ah-an excuse to bub-borrow your car last week. He was, of course, under pup-professional tuh-twenty-four-hour surveillance by this time. He pa-parked in a convenient lay-by near Ely and c-carefully cah-concealed his ill-illicitly acquired pup-plunder. F-fortunately for our chaps, there was room in the l-lay-by for another veh-vehicle and their c-cunningly c-concealed c- cameras c-c-c-captured c-comprehensively all that D-David d-did that d-day. C- consequently, the mum-motor cyclists who so recently accompanied you on the latter p-part of your journey here, are, even as we s-s-speak recovering the inter- na-nationally impor-portant p-papers from where D-David so c-creatively c- concealed them in your magnificent sports car. You're lovely red c-car is currently being s-serviced, w-w-washed, vah-valeted and re-fuelled. If you care to look at the suh-screen on the wall to your left, you will s-see exactly what I mu-mean. Within the hour it will b-be bub-back p-precisely where you left it. Very n-naughty of D-David, of course. U-unforgiveable. We had been actively wuh-working to pah-persuade him to ah-hmm... But he was not really being ah-a very c-cooperative operative."

Smiling smugly at his own juvenile joke, he spreads his hands wide, like a Mafia godfather or a stage magician. The smile disappears.

"You do see, don't you? Steps had to be taken. I do ho-hope you will not allow this unfor-fortunate incident to interfere with your tut-training schedule, Mrs Ingram.

Condescending bastard; a bit like my old headmaster at Roedean.

"That was a pretty smooth manoeuvre you pulled back on the autoroute, Mrs Ingram. Very professional. How do you take your sherry?"

She suppresses the bile that rises in her throat.

Sherry? Sherry? *David's lying there, stone effing dead among the effing dustbins and he probably ordered it. Now, he's asking how I like my effing sherry.*

She's screaming inside. In her calmest, most professional voice, she says primly, *"I'd prefer your driest Martini, if you please, Mr Robertshaw."* Forces herself not to add *'shaken, not stirred'*.

Internal, suppressed, hysterical giggle.

"You do see, don't you Mrs Ingram? We had no ah – n-no alternative. D- David had become ah-a s-serious s-s-security risk. Tut-tut-termination w-was inevitable.

"The verdict will be an unfortunate fall from your fourth floor flat, through faulty fenestration."

She gapes as he rattles off the whole of his last sentence without faltering.

"Yes, yes. Quite." Bristly Moustache's mouse is active again.

"I assure you Mrs Ingwam, his neck was appwowpwiately bwoken. Quite painless d'you know. No, no, he wouldn't feel a thing. He will look absolutely nawmal, if you wish to visit him in the Chapel of West. Such a good man at his job, don't you know. Oh, no. You don't know. Do you. So many of our chaps d'you know… Occupational hazard, you could say."

The mouse rests…

"Yaw pension wights won't be affected, you know."

The mouse takes a nap…

"No long service emolument, I'm afwaid."

She stares at the mouse in fascinated disbelief.

Bloody hell! *Does he mean that as a joke?*

"Natuwally, since he gave his life in service to his countwy, it is only appwowpwiate you should weceive the pwemium pension permitted under the wegulations."

The mouse mesmerises her. The incidence of its nervous twitch seems exponentially proportionate to the agitation apparent in its owner.

"Though I suppose that will be no consola…"

O o h my G o o o d. How did I get here? What's going o o on…? Aahhh! I can't breathe…

She feels her sanity swiftly slipping away. Reaches out to take the Martini proffered by the claw that, earlier, she had, considerately, left attached to the end of its flesh-tinted stick that now was enclosed in charcoal grey, gentlemen's smart suiting…

Shit! What's this? It's not a cocktail gla…

She blinks, blearily, at the bottle in her hand. *Zubrowka Bison Vodka.* The Polish girls at the factory bring it with them in their luggage every year when they come back from their summer holidays. They've taught her to add lime and mint for a Polish mojito.

Trouble is, it always gives me the wildest, weirdest dreams. All jumbled up, they are. Never make any sense. Such a pity David always has to die. And no-one ever uses my first name. How odd. Perhaps it's because I'm a mid-fifties matron.

She pushes the dead bottle under the bed, where it can rest in peace with the others. Stands up from the bed, yawning, stretching, crotch-scratching. She can see Sammy, their snow-white Sealyham, out on the hanky of a lawn, greeting the postman in his usual, noisy way.

Oh well. Another bloody day at the turkey factory, I suppose.

She struggles with the zip on her jeans.

Why does life have to be so bloody dull? In this damp, dingy, duplex in Clapton? Faulty fourth-floor effing fenestration indeed! Huh. I should cocoa.

She scoops the coffee granules into her mug. Two slices of supermarket white into the toaster. Puts the butter and Robertson's on the table. Adds the makings for her first spliff, ready for later. Cocks an eye at the clock on the cooker. David left hours ago. Before daylight.

> *By now he'll be driving his*
> *big six-wheeler,*

scarlet-painted,
London Transport,
diesel engined,

ninety-seven

horsepower omnibus

down

Streatham High Road*

She hums the tune, lightly, as the kettle whistles. The toaster pops. She butters the toast lavishly. Life could be a lot worse, she supposes, spreading the Robertshaw's. Smiles to herself, at her little, private joke. Gets up from the table. Lights the spliff, taking a long, hard pull, deep into her lungs.

So convenient, growing our own in the little greenhouse round the back. I wonder what a 'Pukka Saab' is…Perhaps it's their new 4 x 4…

~~~~~~

*With acknowledgement to Michael Flanders and Donald Swan.

LUNAR LANDING

STU WICKEN'S STORY

From the time of my conception, concerning which my late father, it's alleged, would relate lewd anecdotes through the drifting cigar smoke at the Mess dinner table after his third glass of port, he liked to tell me I was destined to follow a military career. Back in the Civil War (American, of course) a number of my ancestors distinguished themselves militarily, alongside the unfortunate Stonewall Jackson and, later, at Gettysburg, in support of the Southern Confederacy. Even before that my family saw decades of military service; indeed, we were active participants in Wellington's victory at Waterloo. Dad never tired of assuring me (and indeed anyone else on whom he could achieve his customary verbal armlock):

"There was a Wickens with Wellington at Waterloo, dear boy. Don't you ever forget that."

By the time the US got involved in World War I in April 1917, my Granddaddy was known in his regiment as Colonel (later General) 'Warring' Warwick Wickens. My father also, as recorded in the annals of his regiment, did well, achieving no little fame in his front-line shenanigans – as well as the field rank of Brigadier General – under 'Ike' Eisenhower in the European zone of World War II.

Even as a kid, I had other ideas. I got one of my school buddies to smuggle me his copies of Jane's Aircraft and I studied them methodically while dutifully treading Papa's prescribed pre-West Point educational pathway.

Alas, my parentally envisaged transition from college to West Point, seamlessly certain though it was anticipated to have been, never came to pass. Poor Papa, perilously apoplectic in his protestations, passed unpeacefully away the day I tried to explain how my aeronautical, even astronautical, ambitions had led me to enrol in the United States Air Force. Places at that officers' training establishment were reserved in advance by earlier generations, rather in the manner of pre-booking your anticipated offspring's burial plot in the bloody cemetery. Cancellation caused considerable consternation. Not to mention shock tremors in the Mess.

The last intelligible words I heard pass poor Papa's blue lips as he lay, panting, features contorted in rage, body violently tensed in fury, on his army cot (he always refused to sleep in an ordinary bed [although it seems reasonable to suppose he must have visited dear Mama from time to time]) were frightening in the intensity of their delivery:

"I disown you as my son… … Damn you, boy. You are no longer my son and heir … … traitorous, deceitful … … Bring me my service revolver and I'll … … I'll shoot you for the treacherous … aah … cowardly ugh, deserter that … … Arrgh."

Happily, these infamous last words, never before published, in no way adversely influenced the flying career on which I was now launched (and upon which my familial history undoubtedly had some influence) so that my progress through faster and faster Air Force jets (as well as documented action in a couple of the world's armed conflicts) inevitably led me to the notorious precincts of fabled secrecy and mystery. Area 51.

Although we were all highly academically qualified, good IQ scores and all that stuff, as well as having much relevant aeronautical experience, astronautics was, for everyone, a whole new ballgame. Over a decade, while keeping our hand in with flying sub-sonic, supersonic, not to mention super high-altitude spy planes, staying in touch with rapidly developing technology in aeronautics, aerodynamics and communications stuff, we also played a significant, ineluctable role in the highly secretive development of space travel vehicles, with the declared objective of returning to Mars. The Mars, that is, from which our earliest traceable ancestors arrived on Earth millions of years ago. That's all I'm permitted to say about the technological development work. No doubt in twenty-five years' time, folk'll be saying, 'What's so special, so secret about all that? It didn't work anyway'.

And in the end, it didn't. But in fairness to all, it wasn't for want of trying. And remember the real objective in the minds of the world's global governance groups, as discussed behind the closed doors, was getting back to Mars with a view to returning our whole human race there. Permanently. Why? Because Planet Earth was already being destroyed by humankind and soon, unless they leave first, *she* will destroy *him*.

A whole lot of space dollars went up into LEO without ever solving the problems of protection from the massive radiation doses encountered at the higher altitudes. The vehicles were experiencing material damage, electrical and electronic equipment suffered a high incidence of malfunction due to radiation-induced damage and deterioration. Time came, NASA & Co could suppress it no longer – at least within its own corridors. We were working in close collaboration with the Russians on this. The metallurgists had no solution. The astrophysicists likewise. Inter-disciplinary boundaries and historical classifications were dismantled and maximum inter-departmental cooperation demanded from all concerned, in East and West – to no avail.

Urgent top-secret high-level exchanges must have been going on but, you know what they say about pay-grades. Us guys who were flying their bloody machines didn't have a clue.

Seems it was agreed, at top level, for all word of these international exchanges to be suppressed, like so much other stuff. It was also agreed that, because it couldn't be done in anything like the intended time-scale, the US should be the ones to broadcast, in due course, their hoax with Apollo 12 while the USSR, in the kind of secrecy only they were capable of enforcing, carried out a parallel programme.

By the early 1960s the general public on both sides of the Atlantic were getting quite excited as the information reaching them through the news media and scientific journals suggested that quite soon …

Nevada Evening News, September 28th 1961, page 2.

By Umberto P Uranus, Chief Space Reporter.

The head of NASA is said to have been very upset when assessing   progress reports at a Planning Meeting in Area 51 –

"Okay, let's do the Moon first, guys, just for some practice; you know,   get our hand in. We can do Mars later. Yeah, I'll let Mr President know.   Guess he'll be as disappointed as we are."

*

So, the US did it. Only a limited few, even in NASA and Area 51 knew the truth. Obnoxious as the despicable deception was, it was easily orchestrated. The majority of NASA, Area 51 and Baikonur/ Tyuratam personnel were unaware of the duplicity of their masters. Only those intimately involved in preparing and broadcasting the specially produced films and tapes would ever know the truth.

There seemed to be some profound reason why no one was cracking our inability to pass living creatures, including humans, through those goddamned Van Allen Belts. Along with Randy Randolph and a couple of others, I decided to tackle the Padre, a smart guy.

Maybe he had some ideas – none of the domeheads seemed to be getting anywhere. The Padre postulated that for the last 10,000 years, since the last Ice Age, technology advances and the human race's progress coincided pretty closely. He referred to theories about the destruction of Atlantis and the dispersal of humanoid survivors. He suggested this could account for advanced ancient civilisations appearing across the world. He quoted the Egyptians, elsewhere such as black Africa, North, South and Central America, Incas, pre-Mexican Mayas and such like.

The occupants of Area 51 may think they're going to land a man on the moon but the Padre reckoned it jest ain't gonna happen. He voiced thoughts we'd already talked about. What if someone, some unknown, hidden group beyond NASA and the other space agencies, here and in other countries, fully aware that they couldn't send astronauts through the VAB, were proposing a colossal hoax? To show a fully operational launch and the Apollo ship disappearing into space, only to remain in low-earth orbit. Bring the guys back safely in the established routine and no-one else need know. How is this different from any of the other scams in recent centuries? With current film and photography technology, the whole world would be fooled. Unusual stuff to hear from a man of the cloth, but this guy was no ordinary Padre, that's for sure.

Area 51, part of a huge area of the vast Nevada desert reserved for top secret research and testing of supersonic aircraft and development of spacecraft, was pretty hot on security, even back then. Tighter than an *anatidae's anus was our phrase. But with all the build-up they couldn't just say;

"Doh! We can't actually do this can we, fellahs? But we're gonna look such stupid, incompetent fools if we don't do something. Our public expects us to give them something."

So I gave them my two cents' worth:

"Yeah, and now the Russian N-1 bit the dust big-time, it'll only take 'em a year or so to finish the N-2 with the anti-radiation mods and do the real thing from Baikonur, their launch place in Kazakhstan. We've already got boots on the ground there. Keep Buzz, Neill and A. N. Other for the TV show and send me, Will, and Greg to Russia to fly N-2 'cause we already did the conversion course on N1. Randolph can easily do the software programmes, can't you, Randy?"

And so it's all set up. Greg and Will are with me on our way to deepest Russia. I'm glad it's Will, because neither of us leaves a wife behind. Perhaps someday, I'll explain that secret, too. I'll let you know, when I get back, how it all works out.

*

WILL STUART'S STORY

How on earth did I ever metamorphose from the simple, nature-loving son of a deer-stalking, salmon-fishing, golf-club-swinging, eightsome-reel-dancing ghillie on a Royal Estate in Scotland to membership of the elite team of aspiring astronauts in the (nearly) God forsaken vastness of the Nevada desert of North America, surrounded by a bunch of geeks and nerds who speak, (although it is basically Americanised English) a language full of words that the vast majority of the English-speaking world has never heard, and would certainly not understand? Well, it seems a little bit of education goes a long way.

My own unusual form and style of speech, Erse- or Gael- accented-English, is a source of amused, sometimes irritating, communication difficulty among my American colleagues, but I've learned to refrain from its more extreme terminologies and usages, especially when engaged in matters related to The Space Programme, since misunderstandings of not inconsiderable significance have arisen from the 'language problem'.

I can write and speak my native tongue fluently and freely; after all it is the medium of verbal and written communication common in my genetically related community. I acquired my use of English in the form you now read because, at the appropriate stage in my education I won a scholarship according me access to Cambridge University, far away to the south, in

England. There too, I experienced linguistic problematics in written and verbal discourse. At the same time, this taste for the rhythmic cadences and nuances of the spoken word enabled fluency in a number of European languages; finally to the challenging Cyrillic conformations of Russian. I jibbed at Japanese, although I rank it among the most beautiful languages of the world.

It's anomalous in this mid-twentieth century, after all the centuries-long strife between our two nations (I apologise; I refer now not to Russia or Japan but to the conflict concerning acquisition of independence of my homeland from the fettering influence of the [superficially] United Kingdom), that matters of monarchical fealty and religious headship are still vehemently discussed at social gatherings north and south of our jealously maintained border. Tongues, I assure you, are carefully guarded at the annual Ghillies Ball at the Castle, for jobs are hard to come by.

Having seen that border from a height as experienced only by myself and a select few of my astronautical colleagues, I despair of humankind's foolish preoccupation with inter-racial rivalries and landholding disputations, not to mention the minerals beneath the land. At the same time, I'm in awe of the wondrous visual and emotional experience.

While, for most of us, echoes of the Stuart Monarchy and Culloden have faded into nostalgic recollections now only stirred by over-indulgence in the ingestion of *uisce beatha*, better known as the water of life or, more commonly, whisky, there remains the small matter of the Highland Clearances. That century or so of forced evictions of my ancestors from their traditional land holdings and clan-based way of life to make room for sheep-grazing is still the source of bitterly acrimonious, nay, vindictively rancorous (in spite of my linguistically acrobatic qualifications, I confess to some difficulty in translating from the Erse) remarks that burn my ears whenever I return to my origins. To that land of rugged scenery – mountains and waterfalls, large tracts of natural Caledonian Pine afforestation, lochs and lochans; the attendant wildlife, be it the belligerently competitive roar of rutting stags or the wrenching, eventide grieving conversations of loons and divers.

Or even the not-so-wild life. Have you ever stood alone on the shore of a seemingly deserted sea-loch, the only sound the rippling of wavelets as a gentle onshore breeze brushes caressingly across its silvery surface? Startlingly, the near-silence is disturbed by the unique sound of a piper's initial priming of his instrument; suddenly louder as he moves into the opening bars of a haunting, heartstring-tugging lament. Scanning the surface against the dying rays of the setting sun, I spot him, sitting on the gunnel of his rowboat with shipped oars, mourning the passing of … … Tearing up, I turn away. I have no place here, no right to intrude on a poignant moment of someone else's private grief. I … I'm sorry. Just for a moment there I thought I heard …

And then I set that against the hugely wealthy deer-stalking, salmon fishing, golf playing, reel-dancing syndicates that now operate over the vast estates of the Georgian, Victorian and post-Victorian land-owning, whisky-distilling aristocracy.

But enough of my nostalgia. I apologise for my predilection for getting caught up in my own self-inflicted pronouncements, for we can never go back, can we? Only forward.

And now I find myself transplanted, so to speak, from almost mediaeval, beneficence-dependent near poverty to the very forefront of twentieth century technological progress as it ploughs through the multi-billions of dollars of its "budget." Soon, I will go to the moon, or so it is hoped and planned. But, *the best laid schemes o' Mice an' Men, Gang aft agley*, as my fellow-countryman Robert Burns famously wrote.

As I commit my story to the written page, these things remain a tad uncertain. Clearly the intention is undeniable; as to the technical capability, in the face of data returns on discoveries of impedimentary energy fields, I am now less convinced of the glorious success predicted by some who temporarily tenant the higher echelons of political power. Lap o' the gods, someone else said (though I would beg leave to argue that point – but not just now).

In spite of one of the best educations in this world, I confess to some difficulty with the intellectual and ethical contortions required by these present circumstances. After much conscientious self-examination, I've concluded that the problems are more physical than metaphysical. Whatever the moralities, there is a simple material obstacle. It's a question of the ability of the human body to withstand the destructive effects of the energy environment beyond its own planetary envelope. Whether this 'energy' is a random effect of the expanding universe on astral bodies floating freely (though this is open to disputation) within it, or the disciplined effect of application of ordained interaction, principally gravitational, between said bodies, or the decision by some super-natural authority that our planet should remain interspatially isolated from other planetary self-aware lifeforms.

Concurrent with my other Cambridge studies was an interest in astrophysics which contributed, along with my Royal Air Force experiences, to my being selected as an aspiring astronaut. According to the postulations of Dr James Van Allen, there is a zone of radiation surrounding Earth at a distance from eight Earth radii to an as yet unconfirmed distance beyond, which has a terminal effect on mammalian lifeforms, material objects and electrically-operated equipment.

To confirm this, the Americans, during the summer of 1958 detonated three nuclear devices just below the Van Allen belts and monitored the results. The reported results were as I've described.

Back in Blighty, Sir Bernard Lovell & Co. declared themselves 'alarmed' at the observed results. Phrases like 'temporary disruption of the Earth's ionosphere' 'artificially induced aurorae, magnetic storms – fadeout of short-wave communications' were current.

In December 1959, almost ten years before Apollo, American Explorer VII scientists were admitting that sporadic bursts of radiation could "influence" manned space flights. In October 1963, Soviet President Khrushchev, referring to the Americans, prophesied:

"We will see how they fly there, and how they land there and, most important, how they will take off and return."

In spite of the billions of dollars and roubles they're throwing at this, nobody is going through those radiation belts any time soon. A sizeable slice of Area 51's personnel have, metaphorically, put their feet on the desk and look forward to enjoying the occasional LEO ride that comes their way. More than that I cannot say.

*

Well, here we go. Off to Baikonur for, they say, the Big Yin. Stu, Greg and me. We're going to fly this one to the Moon and back.

*

Greg. For God's sake. That's not the Moon we're seeing. That's the Earth – we've seen it before. What's going on? Greg! We can't land this thing on the Earth. Not at this descent rate. Greg!! Someone's messed with the software. Look, that's the Gobi Desert. Randolph's fiddled the camera feeds. Greg, it's all gone crazy. Dammit, slow us down Greg! You're the driver of this rig. Greg …Greg …

*

LUNAR LANDING

Shit! How the hell did this happen?

It should've been a nice, soft, gentle landing on the lunar surface. But it bloody wasn't. It was an almighty, bouncing, bruising bang. Well, sort of.

As I regain consciousness, my scattered wits, I take stock. Shit again, we're not even right fucking way up. Stu, in the other seat, has blood inside his visor. *Stu, Stu. Wake up, man for Chrissake talk to me.* He doesn't answer the intercom. Look at all those flashing fucking lights; the electronics are buggered. Jesus K Rist, we can't get back to the orbiter; I'll never survive … Shit, none of it's working.

"Orbiter One Orbiter One This is Lander Alpha Lander Alpha Do you read me Do you read me? Walt, Walt, for Chrissake man. Walt…Walt!"

Walt's not hearing me. Or if he is, I can't hear him. I hope like hell he's calling Houston: –

"HOUSTON, WE HAVE A FUCKING PROBLEM"

What the fuck can Houston do, three hundred thousand fucking miles away? The only way this has happened is because someone's fucked with the software. Must've been during assembly back at 51. Once the rig left for Baikonur, everything would've been stitched up tighter than the proverbial anatidae's anus**, so tight not even a desert bug, and God knows there's enough of them, could've got at that software. Has to be one of the programmers, though how the … …

All through the months of training and preparation they kept telling us it's impossible. Can. Not. Happen. Theoretically, I know they're right. So why am I lying awkwardly next to Stu's corpse in this wreck of a lunar lander? Corpse? With all that blood on the inside of his visor, Stu can only be dead. Walt, back in the orbiter, must be wondering. I still can't raise him either.

It should've been a simple enough touchdown. Someone's got the math wrong. But that can't be. Unmanned tests were all okay? Manned ones, too.

The more I think about it the more certain I am. Someone's messed with the gravity data for the landing sequence. Houston must know that. Right now, Houston'll be wondering what the fucking hell happened in those last seconds. But someone in Houston knows exactly what's happened. And I've a good idea who that someone is … fucking bastard Randy Randolph, senior programmer. Shouldn't've messed around with his missis. God she's wonderful in bed. Nothing I can do about it now. There's fuck-all Walt can do to get us, either. Wonder if he'll get back okay. Shit, he can't without us.

Three wandering astronauts lost out in space.
Not one of us will get back to base.
Ha, ha, fucking ha!

More I think about it, more I reckon I'd be better off dead, too.

Like Stu.

Like Walt.

Like fucking Randy meant me to be …

And in a few short, unimaginable hours … Don't go there man.

Don't suppose praying'll do much good … *Our Father who art … … …*

Hah! Clever Randy. The world's most expensive funeral in the world's most expensive fucking hearse. NOT. It's the first lunar funeral. And not a loonie moonie mourner in sight.

I'm looking at the little locker that holds the ultimate solution for the stranded astronaut. I even manage a ghost of a smile – that's not exactly what it says on the tidy little, neatly stencilled label.

I…I…ahh… …… aaahh … I can't fucking reach … *Our Father who … Lord Jesus receive my…* Do I really deserve this? Randy you rotten fucking sod, I'll be waiting for you down there among Dante's nine infernal fucking circles … … and when I find you, I'll …

I'm sorry, Beth. I really loved you, back when. It was all falling apart; but at least now you'll never need to know what a rotten traitorous bastard I've been. Mind you, everybody's screwing everybody else down there so what the hell … … … can't … fucking … reach …Can't Ooooh fucking breathe … *Glory be to the Father and to…* … …

National fucking heroes, that's what we'll be. Full triple military funeral, bands from all the services. Huh. God … I can't breathe …

Yes, Mr President, they deserve nothing less. National mourning, Sir? What, three days Sir? A week? Yessir, I'm on it Sir. Nationwide TV Sir? Yessir I'm …

I will present flags and posthumous medals to the grieving wives, Major … Agreed, gentlemen?

… Ooooh … Haaa … My chest …

In the Oval Office, Major, nothing less. Oh! Sir, yessir, yessir, with cameras Sir. It's unprecedented Sir … but yessir, I'm on it Mr President.

God what a meal he'll make of it though. He'll probably sleep with the fucking video under his fucking pillow. Almost wish I could be there … see Beth again … Ooooh – Haaaaaaaaaaaa………..

*

*Of course, it's fiction but I think I may be the last one alive who knows all the facts that have never been made public about NASA and the Apollo series. In Area 51, Nevada, we buried it all so deep – and I don't mean in the sand either – not even subsequent Presidents have ever found it – God knows every one of them's tried. Won't find my computer files, either. But I've fixed it so that, one day, many more years yet, a bank manager, somewhere in Switzerland … So, I'm careful just what I do say. After all, I took the oath, too. I'm only ninety-four – good for a few more yet.

**anatidae's anus, that's duck's ass to most of us. Although the phrase is from the Latin, it was an adoptive Americanism in common usage around Area 51 in the 1960s – as were other offensive words and phrases found above – maybe it's still that way. I don't know. Yeah, it's been a while.

In the interests of realism, I have neither paraphrased nor asterisked those words. At the same time, I think I may have omitted some. The fault for any such inaccuracy is entirely mine.

*

LIFE AND DEATH WITH AN ADULTEROUS ASTRONAUT

Splat!

Half a second ago, it was a perfectly produced Spanish omelette. Now it lies, splattered in shades of yellow, gold and eggy, across the contrasting black tiles of my kitchen floor.

For the thousandth time I curse the day I volunteered to lead my team in defusing the Second World War UXB in the Thames mud right against the bank by Chelsea Flour Mill. Everyone knows there are still hundreds of the damn things in the mud and slime of Europe's rivers and when they do turn up, somebody's got to do it – defuse – make safe – or just blow the bloody things up. For the thousandth time, I remind myself it could've been so much worse. I lost only a hand to a corroded detonator. Some of my former Bomb Disposal Squad mates've lost a whole lot more. I try not to go there. It only makes my throbbing head worse.

The artificial limb people at Roehampton gave me back a right hand – of sorts – and I am left-handed. I've no right to complain. I knew I was choosing a dangerous career, just like Dad. He was a lieutenant in the Royal Engineers, clearing the way for Montgomery and Churchill to cross the Rhine back in

'45. Died clearing a German booby-trapped bridge. Only he messed up on a big one – they didn't find anything to bury; he must have gone down the river with the other debris – fish food, I suppose.

Stop it, Beth. Just stop it. I wish someone would invent some way of operating the fingers and bending the wrist. Hah, probably another twenty-five years before that'll happen.

Breaking eggs with one hand is not difficult. I've done it before and I'll ploddy (sorry I do revert sometimes when I'm cross. In English English it's bloody) well do it again, NOW. Getting the finished article onto the plate hasn't worked out so well this time. But Greg isn't here to witness my latest minor culinary disaster. He's learned to live with occasional outbursts of my frustration. Right now, he's somewhere on the base, along with the other arsey astronauts, probably in Hangar LLT3 testing the landing sequences – again.

Meanwhile, the coffee's cold, the toast's cold and my breakfast's on the floor – again. Shit, what a way to start another lonesome Sunday morning, coming down from the weekend high. Subconsciously reacting to the thought, my still woozy brain starts running Kris Kristofferson's '60s hit song on its endless loop. *(On the Sunday mornin' sidewalk / Wishin' Lord that I was stoned / 'cos there's somethin' in a Sunday / Makes a body feel alone. / And there's nothin' short of dyin' / Half as lonesome as the sound / On the sleepin' city sidewalk /*

Sunday morning comin' down.) God, the tears I've shed to the sound of that.

Another box of eggs from the frigidaire. Dammit! I will get it right this time. More peppers, onions, garlic, olive oil and things … … Wow! It's worked! More coffee to perc, more wholemeal in the toaster. Another solitary breakfast. Ah well, if my cooking went any better I'd probably put weight on. Got to maintain standards.

Guess I'd better – shit, there I go. *I suppose* I'd better clean and tidy up, rearrange the flowers (just try that for one-handed juggling) he likes so much to come home to, when he comes home. And then – I bite back the scream. God, there's nothing else much to do around here. I find sex an intellectually academic subject with little physical appeal. I've never felt any blossoming of maternal instincts so the intended outcome of the biological function has never been allowed to materialise – if you see what I mean. No kids under my feet. Mind you, they'd be in their late teens by now. Too late now anyway, probably. And Greg was never interested so . . .?

I know my disconcerting 'frigidity' hasn't gone unnoticed by the rest of the bitchy, gossiping wives, almost all white American, among whom sex is the predominant conversational topic, so they haven't received me very cordially. 'Coldly calculating' I overheard one of the blowsy bitches asserting. And their eyes. Always furtively looking for my plastic prosthesis. It's an artificial hand – and a pretty poor one at that. I don't much care for the husbands either. I've tried not to look available, but there've been two or three advances, pretty easily brushed off. A bit of clumsy fumbling with the dummy digits and ardour seems to cool quite quickly. The only decent, respectful man is Randy, and he's off-limits because he's married – to a *very* sexy woman. And I'm married too – so that's that.

On the other hand (whoops – Freudian slip?), I used to be pretty, cheerful, optimistic even, but losing the useful bit off the end of my arm changed all that. Here, I'm bored out of my skull. My normally active brain gets very little stimulating exercise these days. Crappy radio and television constantly interrupted by even crappier adverts soon palls. And I'm certainly not looking for social or sexual diversion around here. They'd all be pretty passing and shallow anyway. It's not as if there's any more Brits involved in the programme. Oh, yes. There is one, from somewhere in Scotland I think, but he does rather strangle his English. Will Stuart. He'll be with Greg in the Lunar Lander when (if?) they ever do get to the bloody moon.

Much as I love him (loved him?), I wouldn't have agreed to relocate but Greg insisted it was what 'they' expected of him. Stable relationship, settled home life, no domestic distractions. I could do with distracting right now and it isn't going to be with any of these brash, noisy, self-opinionated Yanks. Yuk!

Oh, to be back in Snowdonia, backpack sitting comfortably, boots fitting likewise, thumb stick snug in my good hand. Or collect Wynny, my Welsh cob, from the trekking centre and spend a whole day riding up into the solitude of the higher peaks and ridges. She's an easy ride, trained for handicapped riders, so a missing hand's not a problem – for her. I love it there with the occasional gust of wind, while the only company is the musical cry of the choughs swirling around the crags. It's a different life in another world. My world. Our world for a while. Oh, Greg! Will we ever get back there?

The ringing phone interrupts my gloomy daydreaming.

"Hey, Bethan Babe!"

Oh God, he's even beginning to sound like one of them.

"Hello Greg, how's your day going?"

I know the answer before it comes. Greg says the line's monitored all day, every day. Security's that damn tight even casual conversation isn't the same any more. (I do love Greg's phrase – it's very down to earth – he says it's tighter than an *anatidae's anus).

"Oh, you know, honey. Same ole, same ole."

He's really going native on me. Even his acquired but usually impeccable Oxford tones that almost conceal his South Walian origins are taking on a transatlantic twang. Does he really want that badly to be one of the guys? Well, I've no intention of being one of the gals. This whole damn space programme thing's spoiling it all. I don't exactly hate all Americans on principle; it's just a pity the *Mayflower* with its cargo of Pilgrim Fathers didn't hit a proper Atlantic storm on the way over. Or a bloody iceberg, like the Titanic. I was so happy with Greg in the early years together, exploring the wilder parts of North Wales and other countries. I drag my thoughts back to the moment. Greg's speaking:

"Guess we're gonna be a bit late again, hon."

His Welsh-Oxford-pseudo-American accent, already discreetly the butt of some humour among our adopted community, is so ugly.

"Very well, cariad. (He hates it when I speak Welsh). I'll just have to cook for one again. I guess."

I can't help adding the little Americanism. I know it sounds silly, and I know it'll niggle him but, what the hell.

"Call ya later, hon."

As I hang up, I remember last night's call. Not from Greg. A female voice, gruffly disguised.

"D'jah know he's cheat'n on yah, sweetheart?"

Dial tone.

So, it is true. Suspicion's been worming into my mind for two or three months now. Just little things that lie between us. Customarily casual conversations cut short. Comfortably familiar words and phrases unsaid. Seemingly accidental but intimate touches – missing. Even our bedtime activities, irregular maybe, now near non-existent. Not that that worries me much – but it used to bother *him*. I've always removed the plastic bit at bed-time but now he seems to shy away from the stump. He rarely touches me.

They say the wronged woman always knows. Now I do know and I realise why the disappointment I've been associating with thoughts of love's dying embers has begun to undermine my usual efforts to maintain an easy-going attitude. It's burning up into something more destructive. Well, maybe it's time to light a fire or two myself, help the destruction get underway.

I load the dishwasher and go out to the patio, easily resisting the urge to build another joint on the grounds that I've never learned how to do it one-handed while standing up. This Area 51's full of the stuff. Marijuana and derivatives thereof, that is. There's plenty of other stuff to be had too, but not for me. I had enough of drugs after my accident. Though I really do find the regular joint therapeutic. Back in Wales most of us smoked spliffs, that is mixing the marijuana, cannabis, rolled with tobacco. The guys here tend towards joints rather than spliffs, probably because of the adverse publicity tobacco's started getting. I've made the transition, it's much better; but even then it's a pleasure I can't share with Greg. They'd be on to him in no time at the base with their blood tests and pee-in-the-bottle-please and so on.

Ahh, what the hell; where'd I put my makings?

*

Shocked as I am, I can't just up and walk out but I've been thinking about Greg and his carryings-on. If I walk out there's all sorts of repercussions. Where's my pen?

1. They'll kick Greg off the Programme (I refuse to write PROGRAM. Shit! I just did.)

2. If I quietly sit tight, be discreet, make no waves, don't let him know about the tip-off; I wonder who it was (is)?

3. I don't actually know who tipped me off *or* who she means.

4. If the husband knows, maybe I can get back at Greg that way. Have to find out who's fucking who first. Word is there's a lot of that about, too. Get the husband to duff him up a bit? Nothing too serious. Just teach him a lesson. Catch him in the act? UGH! revolting idea.

5. They'll not let me leave the country, which seems a good idea – get back to my mountains.

6. They won't even let me leave 51. Might even 'disappear' me if I try. The guys say it's happened before. Don't want that.

7. DON'T WITHDRAW HIS CONJUGAL RIGHTS (I once read, somewhere, this enables the wrongdoer to reverse the roles, or something). Not that he'll worry too much about that if he's getting it elsewhere. He hasn't been so needy lately.

8. Wonder what would happen if *I* started screwing *him* every night. (Irrepressible giggle). Get the cheating bugger exhausted (giggle). It'd ruin his chances of flying the Lander for the space shot two months from now. He wouldn't pass the pre-med. That'd give the rest of them a laugh. Could he keep it up that long? (No pun intended) Could I keep it going that long? Would I want to, knowing

what I know? What would *she* think? I think maybe not. He'd get suspicious (it's never happened before!).

Guess I'll sleep on it for tonight. Can't stop thinking, though.

*

Bloody Hell! Greg hasn't been home all night. What's going on? I can't call him at work – not allowed to distract him. Why didn't he call me? He's allowed that, in a break. Damn, this is getting serious. I'll get the bastard. You just watch me.

No cooking this morning. I hate their bloody breakfast cereals. Too sickly sweet. No wonder the kids are all so roly-bloody-poly. The bread's no better but it'll have to do. The wholemeal's not too bad; it'll have to do for toast if I'm going to eat. Easier than an omelette anyway. Don't know what they do to the bloody coffee either. Ugh, I feel shitty this morning. Didn't sleep that well. No wonder. Ah well. One way or another I'm going to get the sod.

I'm into my second coffee. Rolling a joint. Huh! That's a joke in itself. The house phone rings. Good. Should be Greg. Wonder what he'll have to say for himself. Softly, softly now. Behave normally.

"Hey, Bethan Babe." No exclamation mark.

Oh, no.

"Hello Greg. What have you been up to all night? (That should help things along). Is everything all right? Are you okay? Will you be home for breakfast?"

Anxious little homebird, me.

"No, no, it's okay, babe." (Ugh) "Just a cuppla," (ugh) "hitches in the separation sequence, that's all. Something in the software, they said. Anyway, Randy's spent some time on it. Says he's fixed it so we'll have to do it all again today. Could be another long session."

Yuk! Trouble getting separated? I'll bet. Did he say that on purpose or doesn't he realise how disgustingly suggestive it sounds?

"Very well, Greg. You will keep me posted as to progress, won't you?"

"Sure, sure. It'll be okay. Don't worry about me. I'll call you. Bye."

I'm seriously startled when the phone rings again only a couple of minutes later.

"D'jah know he's cheat'n on yah, sweetheart?"

Same female voice, gruffly disguised. What's going on?

"Yeah, it's me again. I said that so you'd know. I bin thinkin'. If you're plannin' on, you know, maybe stirrin' things up a bit, look no further than the head honcho in Programming."

Dial tone.

My God, this is getting out of hand. Head programmer? Head programmer? Shit! That's Randy, the one nice guy, the one Greg just said was mending software. Randy Randolph – for God's sake! Randy and Gloria. Don't really know him. Can't stand her. That must've been Gloria who called. Is she the other injured party? She did a good job with the voice. Fooled me.

But why would she call *me*? Why would I talk to Randy? What can he do? What's she suggesting he *is* doing? And who with? Shit, she doesn't mean Randy and Greg … surely not that … What the hell's going on? Fornication, adultery, that's one thing. Sort of accepted by the top brass and security, like an occupational hazard among the nerds and geeks around this place. But homosexuality? They'd be down on the guys like a ton of bricks. No way anybody'd get away with that. Dishonourable discharge.

This has me floored – can't get my head round it at all. But what if I'm wrong? What if that wasn't Gloria at all? What if there's another woman who's got the hots for Randy and he's not going for it? So, she calls me to make me think Greg's playing away with Randy. Just to drop them both in the shit? No, I'm overthinking this. Maybe there's a third woman (or is it fourth if you count me?) and Randy's having it off with her. And which one *is* Greg screwing? Is The Voice suggesting I come on to Randy? I don't go in for cheating, even if Greg is.

Now if The Voice had suggested I ask Randy for a *job,* that'd be something actually interesting. I need to get back to work.

It's too much. Third coffee. Another joint. I'm getting nowhere and it's doing my head in; as they've started saying around here. I'll just have to keep my wits about me, try and figure it out. Maybe try a quiet word with Randy. See if I can get anything clear. I've got a first-class brain for electronics, I'm a team player. I could mange a computer better one-handed than a frying pan. But that could make things even worse. Complicate relationships. It's only a couple of months to lift off. Better get things moving. Hahaha, that's a laugh. What comes after love triangle? Love quadrangle? Love pentangle? SEXANGLE Hahaha – ugh. Ooh! my bloody head.

*

Why is everybody being so secretive around here? It's a couple of months now since Greg and the guys flew off to Russia. I'm not supposed to know about that but Greg let it slip at dinner, two nights before they left. He reckons they've shipped an Apollo over there and he and the others are going up in that. Him and Will and Walt. Not just Low Earth Orbit either. He said they were being set up for the Big One – all the way to the moon. To actually land. And bloody come back, I hope. And then I'm going to leave him.

She with the funny voice hasn't called again, nor has anyone from the base. I had a coffee with Randy Randolph. He seemed nervous around me, dunno why. He did show interest in my skillset and talked about 'reviewing my situation after the mission's over' but I haven't found out a thing about Greg and … whoever. At the suggestion Greg might be playing around he gave me a funny look ... concerned, pitying even. He reached out and took my hand, the left one. Then, wordlessly, he got up and left, seemed choked up. Just what the bloody hell is going on? This is getting scary.

Oh, well, what the hell.

I've put the coffee back on. I'll fix another joint to go with … … Christ, the phone made me jump. I've dropped it all …shit …

"Yes, of course this is Bethan Hopkins.

Who is this?

Who are you?

What?

What's crashed?

Where?

On the fucking moon … you're joking me!

Greg said it couldn't … they couldn't … What is this?

Who the fuck *are* you? Sorry, padre, I'm sorry *I'm sorry*.

You're sure? … … But how?

The guys said all the tests were okay … Oh My God … Greg … Randy … Randy?

Padre, will you …can you … Oh Jesus Christ!"

*

'RANDY' RANDOLPH'S STORY

It'd been okay as long as they couldn't get creatures out through the Van Allen Belts *and back* without the radiation burning everything up. We couldn't get out of Earth's planetary bubble. I'd figured there were good reasons why we couldn't and I got to talking to a few of the guys, especially the Padre. Space travel by humans, whether Americans or Russians, could not progress because the Van Allen belts were deliberately put there by the Greater Power – for a reason.

It was fine managing the exit from the geomagnetic field at the interface with the solar winds. That came early on after the German WWII rocket scientists wound up in the States. Once that happened, the dollar took over and things moved along pretty quickly. In no time at all, they were getting unmanned stuff further and further out. Until they realised just what the radiation was doing to the hardware and the software, screwing up the electronics and, later, the mammals.

Guess you all know where the Bible Belt is; it's quite big chunk in the south-east of our great country. I attended and graduated at the University of Alabama in Tuscaloosa. My full name is Ebenezer Samuel Randolph so the other guys had no trouble with a nickname. What good was Ben or Sam when they could poke fun at 'Randy'? (I want you to know that being called

Randy had nothing whatsoever to do with collegiate campus practices of experimental procreational proclivities.) Being as I am the son of a Presbyterian preacher man, I would say I was exposed to a whole lot of Bible thumping in my early years, not to mention some pretty crude ribbing at college. I'm a serious kind of guy. I am aware of the problems of segregation and desegregation factions warring in our State. Recently I was approached by Bobby Shelton to become active in the Klan but I am irrevocably bound to certain religious convictions which include the equality of all the people of the world regardless of their geographical or racial origins. I have my own path to follow.

After graduation with a Masters in Strategic Communication, I became involved in Advanced Communications Technology and enrolled into the United States Air Force. Here my talents quickly led me to the top of the teams working in NASA and Area 51, supporting the high-speed and supersonic pilots who would later become astronauts. As the development of computing and communications technology progressed through their various stages – and at the time we were way ahead of the Russkies – I was drawn more deeply, more intimately, into the space projects. I guess we all shared the euphoric elation of achievement and the depressing disappointment of the frequent failures the program encountered. By the start of the Apollo series I had progressed to Head of Programing for the software that went into our onboard computers on the orbiter and lander modules. In this, as in all aspects of the job, everything was rigidly compartmentalised, so that left hands and right hands, just occasionally, lost sight of each other. After some indoctrination, swearing of oaths and signing of documents I was made aware that, somewhere way above my pay grade, there was a lot of swapping and sharing going on between ourselves and the Russians. Unavoidably, this along with my progressive realisation of the technological implications and applications of my work was reflected in the development of my inner persona with its lifelong spiritual aspect.

Recognition of the clash between my religious tenets and the doctrines coming out of the Communist regime and their implicit applicability to space travel, was one thing. But disillusion with The American Dream was worse. Realisation came to me most forcibly with the well-documented human and hardware disasters that occurred quite early in the Apollo program. My first specific action didn't come until it hit me – we were going too far. Trying to run before we could even properly stand, never mind walk.

I got to thinking about this. All the time. It became obsessive. I could – should – do something about this. We weren't meant to do this space travel thing. Humankind's place is where we were put in the overall plan of Creation. Maybe it was okay for folks from other places to come and visit Earth but even that hadn't gone right at Roswell and other undisclosed locations. And though we knew there were survivors, secretly housed and working in Area 51 and NASA HQ, at my level of operations we neither saw nor had any contact with them. But sightings have persisted, and coverups have too.

Then they told us the techies (or the Ets) had figured out the radiation protection problem. In Russia, they sent up another (American) test rocket, with livestock. Working with my team's software programing it orbited the moon, dropped a lander (no livestock) which they couldn't retrieve because it was unmanned and we hadn't yet figured out how to do that, and returned intact. The United States didn't tell the world we knew about this activity because, at that level, we were in cahoots with the Russkies and if the rest of the world got to know that, whew! Now it was all systems go for the real thing – a manned lunar landing.

But what could I do? My thinking eventually came down to this:

While acknowledging my actions could   be interpreted as a usurping of Divine Power in a deed comparable with that of Lucifer and the other Fallen Angels, nevertheless I am being shown these things. I am an Elected One. One who must explain and demonstrate to the human race why Man cannot advance inter-planetary and inter-galactic travel at this time. It's why the Van Allen radiation belts were put where they are, by the   responsible Other-dimensional Creation-activating Hierarchical Angels in accordance with their instructions from the All-creating Super Intelligence – He for whom the earthling Hebrews, the chosen race, of whom I am not one, have the Seventy-two Names of God.

Such instructions stipulate that any planet to be constructed for occupancy by self-aware beings in any solar system of the Milky Way Galaxy be encapsulated by an energy shield for the express purpose of confining and containing inhabiting lifeforms. Thus we, the current human occupiers do not have the power or authority to contravene the workings of the Angelic Hierarchy. Therefore, in order to compel the governing powers of Planet Earth to reschedule earthly priorities, the current worldwide space exploration programs must be halted before the PNRDDAD (Point of No Return Detection Device in another Dimension) activates the GIASM (Galactic Integrated Automatic Self-Preservation Mechanism) thereby destroying the presently-resident human lifeform, thus necessitating subsequent planetary recolonization.

Yeah, it's been done before. Atlantis and Lemuria are the most recent, and at least four seriously intelligent humanoid life forms before that. It happens every 25,920 or so years, so that only covers the last 150,000 years, and it sure as heck has been going on a lot longer than that. They reckon its according to our solar system going through energy changes with each transit through its elliptical orbit within the Milky Way, but heck, I'm no astrophysicist.

Then came the bombshell. We were going to send up two Apollo moon shots. *On the same day*. One from

Canaveral and the other, in super-top-secrecy, from the Russian launch site at Tyuratam, Kazakhstan. The US vehicle would go into low-earth orbit while the world watched the high-tech edited 'show' including the famous HOUSTON WE HAVE A PROBLEM and ONE GIANT STEP stuff on its TV screens. The Russian shot, American manufactured but assembled in Russia, would go for the full works – landing, recovery and return. I and my team would program all the computing software for both shots – one for real and one for fun. Yeah, the Russkies were way behind us on all this stuff; their top brass were indulging in their own petty power fights and getting nothing done.

I searched my heart and my conscience as my immediate reaction was horror. Anyway, following my customary meditation practices, I was shown the next, irrevocable step. I was being asked to commit an act of multiple homicide. 'They' told me it was not a culpable contravention of current Christian Convention since it was for a Hierarchical purpose. It sure felt culpable. I did it.

As Head of Programming, I supervised and was hands-on-involved with the work of all my Department. I had access to a lot of the Russian stuff too. I had the means at my disposal. I'd already taken the first steps.

It was I who detonated the earlier Apollo ship on the launchpad, destroying the ship and its occupants. It should have been enough. Guess all the world saw that one but, whatever they all saw, its meaning as a warning got through to no-one. No-one reads the signs anymore. God and His Angels are but things of myth and legend. Man thinks he's in charge. He does what he likes without recognising either his own nature or his place in the Universe. Does he think he can command that, too?

There was a big one coming up and I would be shown what to do.

*

I had to do some serious investigation work, but I was being guided – shown every step of the path ahead of me. And the Padre supported me.

Probably the biggest secret in the whole of the space development thing was that all through the Cold War, as well as long before and still the case, in spite of the posturing of the supposed world leaders, there was another, a hidden agenda conducted by a higher, unseen tier of world domination and control; GGG – the Global Governance Group. They saw things quite differently.

During the last 10,000 years, since the last Ice Age, technological advances have coincided pretty closely with landmark occurrences in civilisation's progress. They took account of the widely accepted scenario of the destruction of Atlantis and dispersal of survivors, which would account for the appearance of advanced civilisations right across our planet. As indicated for example, by architectural and hieroglyphic evidence of ancient Egyptian, Far Eastern, Angkor Watt, Chinese, native North American, South American Incan, pre-Mexican Mayan activities. And that's only since the last

Ice Age. There've been at least four earth-occupying advanced civilisations from as long as ten million years ago. Major cataclysmic events leaving no evidence of their passing, they have remained hidden. Until now. Modern research technologies and equipment are opening new doors to the past.

As a result – growing evidence of visits from so-called 'aliens' – extra-terrestrial beings. Carefully confused information and disinformation regarding the rigged scenarios of the Roswell Incident and other ET landings, as released by the US and world governments, stories of human kidnapping by ET visitors, widespread animal mutilations. All orchestrated by the few ET survivors and the GGG.

Meanwhile, in Area 51? The occupants may think they're participants in the race to land a man on the moon, but consider how easy it would be, after all the recorded and filmed preparations, if someone beyond NASA and other space agencies, already fully aware that they could *not* send astronauts through the VAB, were proposing to broadcast a prepared, edited version of those recordings, while an Apollo ship was jollying around in LEO – low earth orbit. Bring the guys back safely and no-one else need know until decades later, when NASA and the rest have figured out the radiation problem.

Carefully organised scenarios, meticulous scripting, planning, selection of the right 'need to know' group, duck-ass tight security, and it was no different from any of the other scams run at top level in recent centuries. I think it could be done. I decided to have another talk with the Padre.

'Hey', he said, 'just look at the crucifixion and resurrection scenario a couple of thousand years ago and the conspiracy theories around how that was rigged and the body spirited away by Joseph of Arimathea. What do they really know about the Knights Templar and what went on – what they found – under the Temple in Jerusalem? And that chapel place in Scotland with the funny pillars and family connections? There's far too much we don't know. Because somebody doesn't want us to know.'

'With current technology, the whole world can be duped. In any case,' went on the Padre, 'if earlier, Biblical, history is going to be repeated, man is not going to the moon or anywhere else in the solar system until those extra-terrestrial or angelic beings who run the show decide humanity, not a few men, is ready. Current Earth races are so self-centred they haven't even understood how to treat their present domiciliary planet so they can't be turned loose to go tripping off elsewhere. Basic planet-human interdependence, interrelationships, inter-action and understanding of the concurrency of their evolutionary progress will have to develop much further before even the GGG will be granted access to things like the solution to global entrapment by radiation.'

Man, he was some Padre, that guy. He was way ahead of me. But it turned out we were both behind the times.

My part is easy really. The software for the US shot doesn't need to include the lunar landing and recovery stuff. For the Russian shot, to be crewed by Will Stuart, Stu Wickens and Greg Hopkins, just make sure their Lander hits the lunar surface faster than in the practice runs in Hangar LLT3. I have one or two other ideas I'm working on, too. The evidence will be badly damaged if not destroyed. They won't send another one up to get the guys or the gear. No-one will know how or why it happened but it'll sure as heck give GGG cause to pause in their activities. They'll probably accept the perfectly feasible explanation of VAB damage to the Landing Sequence electronics. As for the three astronaut crewmen, they are, regrettably, unavoidable collateral damage. Pretty damned expensive funeral though, if you ask me. Sorry, bad taste. Commiserations to their wives, of course, but I only know one well. Actually, I kinda know her a mite too well.

Oh, I don't mean ... She's just different, that's all, Bethan, sweet lady. Attentive, observant, clever with her shortcomings. Greg's often boasted of her bravery medal, talks less about her artificial hand. It's a shame they couldn't have found a job for a first-class mind like hers.

She came to me one day, asked me if I thought Greg was 'playing around' with anyone. God knows, I thought, they all seem to be at it. The guys want release from tension, and the wives just want attention. Bethan and I have similar problems. When I enter a room with Gloria, it's all eyes on us, every time. I hope she's happy. She spends a lot of time with the other women, keeps the home comfortable and welcoming – that seems to be enough for her. Pity she didn't want kids. But if we'd had them, I would have been torn between work and home. As it is, Gloria demands nothing from me.

Someone, along with the padre, will have to step up and help Bethan in her grief.

So too will the President, in his own inimitable way. He's said to be good with the ladies, whatever that means.

For now, though, all I can do is keep my cool. Just watch and wait.

*

I'm in the Rest Facility at Baikonur when I get the call.

*

If I have got it wrong, my Maker will judge me.

*

THE PADRE'S STORY

I'm Area 51's strangest mystery, only no-one in this vast area of Nevada's desert knows exactly who I am or where I came from. Truth to tell, nor do I. Well, no, that's not quite the whole truth. I know I have a job to do. And no-one, inside or outside this top-secret complex, knows why I'm here – what my secret mission really is. They call me The Padre. Which means I deal in the unknowable, the mysterious, and the best for humankind. Like all pastors (except those failing in their vocation, which does happen), I try to comfort the afflicted, explain the inexplicable, to patrol the areas beyond the understanding of science. I live on the margins of spiritual understanding, well beyond them for most 'spiritual' people, in fact. I am just a bit 'different'.

Earthbound humans tend to focus on the concrete, the understandable, and that includes mainstream churches and theologians. Organisations which dare to assert understanding of the unknowable tend to get pushed out, even when transparent in their dealings, and parading no demagogues who just need access to their followers' wallets to save the world. Unless you are a well-established member of the Spiritualist Movement (to which Movement membership is freely available), you almost certainly know nothing about the cosmic phenomenon that accounts for our presence here.

In the matter of Creation of All, there are, among other Created or Spiritual Beings, those delegated from On High to perform lesser tasks for the perpetuation of the eternal cycle. Within each of the many Created Universes are innumerable galaxies, within which are numerous solar systems. Within the Planetary structure of each such system there is at least one whereon exists an occupying self-aware life form. Allocated to the care and guidance of the Spiritual Evolution of each such Planet and its life form is a group drawn from those sent as Guardians from On High. In respect of each and any such Planet, wherever physically located within its galaxy, this delegated group is the Planetary Angelic Hierarchy. Within each solar system there may or may not be a Planet where the self-aware life-form may or may not be granted the privilege of Free Will.

On any Planet where the occupying self-aware race has abused the privilege of Free Will for purposes embracing self-gratification in its many variations, that Planet's Angelic Hierarchy may deem some intervention necessary. But there are some pretty strict rules governing this. One such rule prohibits direct use by an Angelic Hierarchy of the Cosmic Energy for the purpose of executing such intervention in contravention of the Principle of Free Will. Humans cannot grasp the reasons for this – hence the 'why does God allow suffering?' cliché trotted out by scientific materialists, those who trust only the immediately verifiable in the most shallow terms.

Time is a complexifying influence in the interaction between the high vibratory levels of Cosmic Energy and the much-reduced levels of energy applicable to the third dimensional characteristics of a planet such as Earth. But there are mechanisms for deployment in certain scenarios. Such as that envisaged.

Perhaps the reader is beginning to glimpse my role?

Yes, that's right.

There are no more than twelve of us on Planet Earth at any one time and our job is to follow orders, trusting that the On High never wills harm. But Others do. You may see this opposition in any planetary catastrophe. Wherever there is war, plague, natural disaster, suffering of any kind, an opposing wave of spiritual and practical healing rises up in the populace of that planet. This blue planet, like so many before it, contains both the best and worst, potential for its own destruction. There is ceaseless vigilance from On High against humans blowing themselves up, or, I foresee in the next century, simply overheating themselves out of existence in their careless greed for profit. Creational Law seeks always to balance the consequences of Free Will against healthful wholeness.

In order that you recognise my present situation and the human activity that's about to ensue, you must understand the procedure. In a ceremonial practice, the detailed description of which has no place here, an already incarnate human is permitted to agree to evacuate their spiritual essence (soul) from their physical vehicle and return it to whence they/it originated, there to await a later reincarnation. In instantaneously effective simultaneity, another soul, voluntarily and with Angelic Hierarchical approval, may enter and take possession of that physical vehicle in order to execute a task which will be spiritually relayed to him during the remaining lifetime of that vehicle. But we will, as a result of being confined within that body, be subject to the limitations of its powers, physical and mental. Jesus, to take one example, had the same problem, and its consequences.

Conscious awareness of that phenomenon entering the minds of fellow humans (in this case), isn't allowed, for obvious reasons. Inklings of our role in human affairs did permeate writings millennia ago, with 'angels' and 'gods' described interfering in the affairs of humans in ridiculous fashion. We managed to suppress these insights culturally. But now I am permitted to reveal to those who have the desire to know, (for there will always be those who hide in the blinkers of ignorance) that is who I am and that is whence I came – to carry out a task in respect of undesirable human activity, in contravention of Creational Law, within Area 51 and Planetarily-related geographical locations.

The nominal label of 'Area 51' and what goes on here under that title includes development of rocketry and other propulsionary enablement for extra-planetary exploration with, inevitably, potential for weaponry delivery. The scientists, with their complete incomprehension of the potential disastrous consequences, have perfected ultra-high-speed travel within the Earth's gravitational influence and now, beyond that, into the Cosmos.

There are some other Men of God (yes all male; in spite of its scientific developments this planet has not yet evolved much) with whom I associate freely though rarely together, officially offering 'religious' guidance to the several thousand personnel, their wives and families, manning (note the linguistic perseverance in gender stereotyping) varied higher-than-top-secret functions.

There's a Jesuit priest who trained in Spain and spent the early years of his ministry on the Spanish Balearic island of his birth, Mallorca. He's told me of the small town of Petra where there's a massive and splendid stone cathedral with some remarkable stained glass. It's dedicated to Junipero Serra, described as one 'born to the Light', who became a missionary, founding much of California, apparently. Before coming here to serve Area 51's Catholics, this Jesuit priest had followed Serra's footsteps to South America where he carried on the work of his missionary predecessor. He has done good working among the world's poor. The Christian Church is too preoccupied with trying to induce the rich of this planet to care for their poor to bother much with space travel.

Another is a Jewish Rabbi, for there are many here who follow the beliefs, the ceremonial and liturgical practices of that ancient religion. Yes, they once recognised our existence and interventions in their affairs as 'those whom God has chosen'. Commerce, industry, the Arts, politics, sport, the military, not to mention the Space Race – all are heavily permeated with this formerly Middle Eastern race who are a powerful, influential force at all levels. The forces of evil tried to exterminate them, a huge tragedy, but they have endured. Many maintain their religious path and some, apparently aware of the supposedly 'secret' ET landings, have within my hearing expressed their doubts as to the propriety of seeking a space-travel and domination capability. Their God, the Rabbi tells me, is displeased but, because they find nothing in their Talmud authorising interference, they don't know what to do about it. They still hope for someone to arise among them to guide them – the Messiah.

Muslims aren't significantly represented here, or Buddhists, Hindus or other world religions. Perhaps if they were, for example if followers of the Tibetan Dalai Lama worked here, the destructive nature of their work might be more obvious to them. For none of these groupings, while there are everywhere references to Beings from elsewhere visiting Earth, can find precedential justification for defying the clear Creational intention of planetary confinement by preventative energy barriers. And, as the Jesuit and the Rabbi agree, most workers in Area 51 can use the catch-all 'Science' as a new religion to justify anything they care to pursue, in this case the conquest of Space.

Rumblings and reports of rumblings within these religion-based groups have reached my ears. Even among the astronauts themselves, doubts are being discussed as to the ultimate morality of the situation in which they find themselves. Who is responsible for the haste in pursuing this inordinately costly, (in resources and human life) Program? What is their motivation? Can we, each one of us, with hand on heart, justify our willing participation? Most especially now that we know about the Van Allen radiation belts which were responsible for the failure of purpose of the USA Explorer X satellite back in '61, at around 60,000 miles out, about a fifth of the way to the moon.

The disastrous effects of massive high-level nuclear detonations authorised from the highest levels of government ought to have been sufficient warning. But they were self-evidently for aggressive purposes, so were quickly shut down. Space travel purports to spread civilisation, just as Junipero Serra believed he was spreading civilisation in the Americas, while his fellow explorers spread disease, conquest and exploitation.

The guys talk to me. They're uneasy about the whole thing. I wouldn't exactly say mutinous, but I am doing the job I'm here for. It will be stopped.

I've met Ebenezer Samuel Randolph, a senior figure involved with the programming of computer software on the Program. He doesn't discuss that with me, but he is of religious bent and I've spent much time guiding him in his soul-searching for the moral validity of aspects of the

Space Program. We agree that high-speed, high-altitude spy planes and talk of development of embryonic unmanned drones for use in air-to-ground warfare must be confined to Earth. Whether or not he approves of the morality of those activities is still under discussion. There are angles to the Conquest of Space Program, as some call it, that raise all sorts of ethical issues, questions as to the intentions of upper echelons of worldwide governments.

I try to avoid too much contact with very senior ranks and make good use of my anonymity to keep track of what's going on hereabouts. From time to time, one or another of the thirty astronauts on the project comes to me to unburden himself of his reactions to what they've all experienced during low earth orbits (LEO they call it – 99 to 1,200 miles from the Earth is the furthest extent to which manned spacecraft have so far, successfully travelled and returned). These guys speak in awe of their dawning perspective on humans and our place in Creation.

There's a huge disconnect between these life-changing experience and the way most people here choose to pass their time. I know from the wives that marriage breakdown is common, and the pain this causes women, often with too little to do here already, is going to be difficult to put behind them when this madness is over.

Excuse me, that's my telephone. Hello. Yes. What? Crashed? Where? On the moon? Are you crazy? That's impossible. They can't… … What? From Baikonur? But how? You sure of this, General? I can't believe it. Yes, sir, I'll start making the calls, right away.

*

Hello. Bethan? Yes, it's very bad news I'm afraid. Yes, the one that went up from Baikonur. Yes, all of them. Walt, Stu and your husband. Yes, actually on the Moon. No, no-one could get back. Yes, General Wattis says the military will organise and coordinate everything. I'm so sorry, Bethan … … Would you like me to come over later? I must make some more calls first … … Yes, my dear … you still have so much to live for.

*

JOB DONE
Soon I too will be called back to whence I came … as are we all.

*

JOYCE and ME

My wife Joyce passed from this life at the end of June, 2015.

Over half a century ago we left behind the formal, organised religions and became what some call Spiritual Investigators. From time to time we attended Spiritualist Church meetings wherever we happened to be in the world. Hardly surprising then that, after Joyce's passing, I resumed that practice in our home town.

When I returned home from church that Friday, soon after her passing, I was still on a high. Joyce, of whom some of the others, shall I say, 'became aware', was still with me. I know that because, as I prepared for bed, I put Classic FM on the bedside radio as usual, something we had done for many years. As I snuggled down alone...alone?... I realised 'they' were playing one of Joyce's favourite pieces of music: the 'Elvira Madigan' film music, Mozart's piano concerto No. 21, slow movement. "Oh, nice one," I thought and thanked her again for what had happened an hour or two earlier. I settled down. Closed my eyes and relaxed.

The very next piece was James Horner's film theme from *Titanic*, 'An Ocean of Memories'. What could I do? I cried.

We had been married just over sixty years and, for the latter half of that, we had travelled the world together, by land, sea and air. We had visited all the continents except Antarctica. We had been stony broke, though not actually bankrupt. Afterwards, we made what I can only describe as a small fortune. An Ocean of Memories?

Perhaps I'll tell you about that another time.

Much of the tens of thousands we have spent has financed our world travels so that we could help to heal the earth. Yes, that's right, heal the earth.

Perhaps I'll tell you about that another time.

Yet, there is enough left that, with all our children housed and provided for, (although they are all three childless) when the last one goes, there will be, perhaps, a million pounds bequeathed to Save the Children and other charities.

Instead of going to sleep, I sat up in bed and began writing this. Close to 4 a.m., I put it down – a long way from finished but, I now understood what Joyce had been trying to tell me for decades – WRITE IT DOWN AND SHARE IT.

A few of you have heard snatches of this already because since I recommended attending Spiritualist meetings, I've been trying to share how I use the energies with which I've been gifted – who I am. A healer. All my life I've tried to avoid that label. Joyce knew I was a shy, retiring violet, but that Friday evening with the help of those present, she finally came through and hit me where it hurt. Emotionally, in my heart with her love and metaphorically, in the butt with her boot. I knew from the manner of her passing that, after all those years at my side, she had deliberately taken herself out of my way. From now on, it would be different – I was on my own for the remainder of my mortal life.

Now it is time for me to share.

In the last four years or so of her time here, Joyce experienced Alzheimer's disease. I won't dwell on it but, as some of you undoubtedly know, it is a devastating experience for both sufferer and carer. I, who had been thanked by many for helping them to access healing energies in their own lives, could do nothing, I thought, for this dearest person. Towards the end, while she was still, occasionally, lucid, occasional glimpses of her old sharpness of mind and thought would re-appear. The twenty-four-hour care responsibility had worn me to a state of imminent breakdown, and I could not even care for myself any more. The doctors prescribed serious rest for me and a Care Home for Joyce. That was to be in Criccieth, sixty miles away.

From this time forward we would no longer share the same space. Sacred shared space transitioned to separateness. Time too, was no longer shared but shrank to empty solitude apart.

Daily pilgrimages. For some that could be a sentence to many years of slow deterioration and a pretty lonely, miserable existence at that. But Joyce, with her deep spirituality, decided otherwise. In fact, she had told me a number of times over the years, especially if we met someone crippled with arthritis or suffering with some other debilitating disease,

"I'm not going to get like that; I shall go when I'm ready."

When I visited, she would say,

"I love you. I want to be with you. Please don't keep me here."

When I wasn't there, she refused to eat, drink or sleep, and she patrolled the corridors for most of the twenty-four hours each day. She had even forgotten her three children's existence. She exhibited many of the recognised symptoms of her disease, including undressing by day and by night and 'borrowing' other people's clothes and shoes. On most visits, she would grasp my arm firmly and walk me up and down the whole time, proclaiming,

"I have to go, I have things to do, I can't stay here."

This marked the time when she made the decision to go. Although she was only there for four weeks, this perceived incarceration seemed to stretch out for years, to her. Me, I wondered how long either of us could endure it.

Each time, I cried, though I tried hard to hide it.

She worked herself into a state of utter physical exhaustion in those four weeks and then she suddenly collapsed. A coma. She lasted only a few more days, without recovering consciousness. I realised afterwards that, on my visits, she had been speaking to me from spirit, even though she had appeared still to be occupying her body, and that she had deliberately hastened her own physical demise, to ease both our sufferings, and those of our children.

In our dining room at home, there hangs an oil painting we brought home from one of our trips to the Far East. It shows an idealised street scene, depicting a community in ancient China. It measures roughly 1m 30cm wide by 60cm high. It's in the wooden frame in which I fixed it with one-and-a-half-inch steel panel pins, some twenty-five to thirty years ago.

To try to give Joyce something of her home environment, we took, among other things, this picture and hung it in her room at the Care Home. After her passing we took it back home and because by this time our eldest son, Adrian, had put a different picture in its place, I propped it against the wall, on a small chest of drawers in our bedroom.

For some years Adrian had passed his obsolete mobile phones on to me so that we could keep in touch when on our travels. Each night at home I plug the phone into its charger at the side of my bed. On the second morning after Joyce's passing, I got up and dressed, picked up my phone, <u>without switching it on,</u> and walked past the picture, towards the door.

Before I reached the door, the picture fell forward with a clatter to the floor and broke part way out of the frame. As I turned to see what was happening, the telephone, on which Adrian had downloaded thousands of tunes, began to play music. A tune I had never heard, sung by David Gray, a male singer, of whom I had never heard, called "THE ONE I LOVE."

Again, I cried.

Do I need to say how I interpreted that little surprise?

A day or two later, I found among Joyce's papers, a single sheet of A4 with, typewritten on it, A Spiritual Poem – Anonymous.

It's actually part of a work by Christina Rossetti.

Perhaps some of you know it, but I would like to read it to you.

When I come to the end of the road

And the sun has set for me,
I want no rites in a gloom filled room.
Why cry for a soul set free?
*

Miss me a little, but not too long
And not with your head bowed low.
Remember the love that once we shared.
Miss me, but let me go.
*

For this is a journey we all must take
And each must go alone.
It's all a part of the Master's plan;
A step on the road to home.
*

When you are lonely and sick at heart,
Go to the friends we know
And bury your sorrows in doing good deeds.

Miss me, but let me go.

*

Again, I cried. Joyce had broken through the stone wall of my grief and loneliness to let me know that I'll never be alone, and that she waits happily for me to join her.

Printed in Great Britain
by Amazon